THE HYDROGEN MURDER

THE HYDROGEN MURDER

•

Camille Minichino

AVALON BOOKS
THOMAS BOUREGY AND COMPANY, INC.
401 LAFAYETTE STREET
NEW YORK, NEW YORK 10003

Library of Congress Catalog Card Number 97-94274
ISBN 0-8034-9268-5

SECOND PRINTING

PRINTED IN THE UNITED STATES OF AMERICA
ON ACID-FREE PAPER
BY HADDON CRAFTSMEN, BLOOMSBURG, PENNSYLVANIA

To my husband, Richard Rufer;
my expert consultant and cousin, Robert Durkin;
and my mentor, Penny Warner.

Prologue

At two o'clock on Tuesday morning, Eric Bensen got into his battered cream-colored Volvo and drove to his lab. He needed one more look at the data before he settled on his course of action.

City traffic does sleep, he thought, as he wound through deserted streets a few miles from Boston, a light fall rain bouncing off his headlights. Eric parked in front of the three-story building he'd been calling home for nearly six years as a physics graduate student and let himself in through the basement. Even in the middle of the night, the corridors were noisy with the whining of generators and the hum of long fluorescent tubes that lined the hallway ceiling. Patterns of tiny red, yellow, and green dots from filaments and standby lamps looked like miniature traffic lights spread at random over the racks of electronics.

Eric walked past dark offices, supply closets, and workshops smelling of acids and graphite. He headed down the ramp to the room that held his gas gun—sixty feet of pistons, valves, and gases encased in metal piping, the heart of his hydrogen research. He flicked on the overhead lights, went to his computer, and picked up the printout from Monday's runs.

Resting the thick sheaf of data on his lap, Eric weighed his choices. He could kill one or two lines in the software program and the annoying result would disappear. Or he could acknowledge the error he and his team had made, retract their journal article, and be responsible for setting ten scientists, including his mentor, back to square one.

Eric took a deep breath and ran his fingers through the small amount of dark brown hair he had left. With a balding head and heavy glasses, he looked much older than his thirty-one years.

Eric was within two months of getting his doctorate and moving on to a real job with a good salary and some free time to put his personal life in order. The ticking of the generic clock on the wall above his desk seemed to grow louder as he thought of his wife's constant nagging about starting a family.

He swiveled around, rotating from side to side in his patched gray vinyl chair. Clockwise, instant recognition in the field of hydrogen research and financial security for life. Counterclockwise, embarrassment and disappointment for him and his colleagues.

Eric heard the ramp door open and saw a figure approaching.

''I thought you'd be here,'' said a familiar voice.

''Well, there's work to do,'' Eric said.

''You're not going to do this to me.''

''What . . . ?''

Eric stopped short and watched, as if in a trance, as the figure moved toward him. His eyes formed a question that he didn't bother to ask. He looked at the gun pointed directly at him and turned back to his computer screen. His fingers brushed the keyboard just before the first shot rang out.

Eric fell to the floor. The sounds of two more shots echoed in his brain.

His chair rocked for a few moments without him, then slowed to a full stop.

Chapter One

I blame my mother for all my character flaws. My inability at fifty-five years of age to decide whether to relax to an old Perry Como album, or ride my exercise bike to operatic drinking songs, can be traced to my first twenty years with Josephine Lamerino.

"You don't like yellow," Josephine would tell me. "You don't want that blouse. It'll only hang in the closet. And forget skating lessons, Gloria. You're not athletic."

Now with an evening free, a rarity since I'd come back to my hometown just north of Boston four months ago, I was like an electron searching for an orbit. I couldn't focus on what I wanted to do. I looked around my newly furnished living room, lined with neat rows of science books, biographies, and an occasional classic. I caught my reflection in the large framed print of a cable car on the highest street in San Francisco, a farewell present from the friends I'd left in California, and straightened up to my full five feet three inches.

Maybe there'll be a murder tonight, I thought. *Something to give me a focus.* Thanks to old friends looking out for my mental health, I'd been asked to help the Revere Police Department on science-related cases. Working on my first and only contract thus far I'd testified as an expert witness in a homicide trial involving a chemist as defendant. I felt a thrill to match my best research day when I was able to decode a formula for liquid tungsten for the homicide detectives. My successfully completed assignment led to proof of industrial espionage as the motive for murder, and I considered myself an official amateur detective, if there were such a thing.

Not exactly what I had in mind when I took early retirement. I'd cleaned out my Berkeley condo and my physics lab, signed for my bonus, and flew east. My only plan was to return to the place I fled thirty years before, right after my fiancé died, and see what it felt like.

I made a private resolution to give it a year, then make a new decision. For someone who had a hard time choosing between "Hot Diggety-Dog" and the opening chorus from *La Traviata*, I'd set a lofty goal for myself.

When my phone rang, I was on my way across new blue-and-white speckled linoleum to the refrigerator, another habit learned from Josephine. When bored or in doubt, have a snack. I was relieved to hear Rose's voice. I didn't really want someone murdered just to make my evening interesting.

"The car's ready," Rose said. "Why don't I drive over and we'll go for coffee. You can finally dump that old Jeep you brought from the West Coast."

Rose was my biggest supporter when I first entertained thoughts of coming home again. We'd gone to grade school and high school together, and had never lost touch. After Revere High, I commuted to college in Boston. Rose went to secretarial school, married our childhood friend Frank Galigani, and had two sons and a daughter before I finished a B.S. in physics. By the time I became Dr. Gloria Lamerino six years later, Galigani's Mortuary was a thriving business.

"This is where you belong," Rose said when I told her I was thinking of moving back to Revere. "Even though it's not the same as when you left."

"You mean it's not half Italian and half Jewish anymore?" I said. I already knew that the last three decades had brought great changes in Revere, with large groups of Asians moving into the old Jewish neighborhood on Shirley Avenue. But if the information I'd gathered from the Internet was correct, the city was still more than ninety percent Caucasian.

Rose laughed and told me Italians were still the majority

group and Luberto's Bakery on Broadway had pastry to die for.

"The cannoli are as good as Josephine's," she'd said, thus providing one more reason for me to return.

Rose even had a plan to help me get started again in Revere. She set me up in the apartment above the funeral home she and Frank operated, and made arrangements to hand down last year's Cadillac. Galigani's Mortuary kept only the newest models in its fleet, so I could count on a great used car deal every October.

While I waited for Rose and my new black luxury car, I looked out my window at the enormous Romanesque church standing less than a quarter of a mile away, outlined in the fading sunlight of early fall. Of all the structures that were part of my youth, St. Anthony's was the only one that had survived the years. My beloved grammar school, the Abraham Lincoln, had burned to the ground, and my crumbling red brick high school was razed and replaced by a more modern facility with much less architectural character.

Worst of all, the giant roller coaster and Ferris wheel, Bluebeard's Palace, and all the other amusements that were part of the two-mile-long Revere Beach Boardwalk were history. Multistory apartment buildings lined the oceanfront property where once there were frozen custard and pizza concessions, carousel horses, and bandstands. I'd driven along the coastline once or twice since returning in June, but still hadn't summoned the courage to take a long slow walk along the stretch of beach and boardwalk where I had my first job, my first kiss, my first inkling that I was a person. *Later,* I told myself, *when it's colder and the crowds of beach-walkers have gone.*

I heard a car drive up and went to the door. Prepared to greet Rose, I saw instead someone I hadn't seen in thirty years. He was wearing a gray-and-black tweed jacket and flannel slacks with a crease as sharp as a laser beam. His arms overflowed with a dozen red roses and a box of Fanny Farmer butter creams, my favorites. My old boyfriend Peter Mastrone, voted best dancer in our high school class.

I stepped back, and with one smooth gesture fluffed my short, curly hair and straightened my faded blue-and-gold Berkeley sweatshirt.

''You look beautiful,'' Peter said.

''I wasn't expecting you,'' I said, glancing at my oldest jeans with a hopeless look.

''If I waited for you to phone, it would be another thirty years,'' Peter said. ''I figure you came back to marry *me* this time.'' His wide grin was familiar and comforting, his wavy hair, mostly gray, a reminder of how my own had changed color since I last saw him.

I breathed in the newly arrived smells of chocolate, flowers, and aftershave and had the sense of being thrown back in time. An old confusion of feelings stirred, as if there were decisions still to be made, or unmade. I tilted my head and smiled.

''Hello, Peter,'' I said. ''Come in.''

In the next few seconds I saw Rose come up the stairs and into my hallway. She didn't seem surprised at Peter's presence, and I made a mental note to ask her about it later. Not much taller than I, but a great deal trimmer in her designer jeans, and without a gray hair on her head, Rose followed Peter into my living room.

''I brought the newspaper with me,'' she said, holding out the *Revere Journal*. ''There's a piece in here about a physicist I remember hearing you talk about, Gloria.''

Peter and I leaned over Rose's shoulder as she pointed to a small grainy photograph of Eric Bensen. *Local Scientist Found Shot to Death,* the caption read.

''Isn't he the one you know from California?'' she asked. ''He was murdered early this morning over at the lab at the end of Charger Street.''

It's a good thing I hadn't decided what to do tonight, I thought. *This evening is out of my hands.*

Chapter Two

It worried me that presented with a new car, an old boyfriend bearing gifts, and a murder, I zeroed in on the murder. After a brief concession to "remember when we . . ." and "whatever happened to the girl who . . ." with Rose and Peter, I got to what really interested me.

"Eric Bensen's research team is the one that may have made the biggest breakthrough yet in metallic hydrogen," I said. "I wonder if that had anything to do with his murder."

"What's metallic hydrogen?" Rose asked.

"And what could it possibly have to do with a murder?" Peter asked.

From their opposite corners of my brand-new blue-gray couch, they both reached into the bowl of pretzels, so I knew their questions were ten percent interest and ninety percent polite. I answered them anyway.

"Remember the articles in *Time* magazine and all the popular literature last month?" I said. "The hydrogen work is connected to superconductivity. The potential for utilities and big business is enormous—one-hundred-percent-efficient power lines and magnetically levitated railroad trains, to name only a couple of hot new technologies."

"From hydrogen?" Peter asked. He was sitting up as straight as he could on the deep corduroy cushions, his hands folded on a napkin in his lap as if he were in Sunday school.

I was impressed at the lengths to which Peter was going to be polite. As a history major in college, with a minor in European languages, he'd never liked anything remotely scientific. And he followed up that distaste with a stunning avoidance of technology. According to Rose, who'd given me updates through the years, Peter still had a rotary dial phone and a black and white television set that he kept hidden in an antique oak cupboard.

I took advantage of the moment.

''We've never been able to produce hydrogen in useful metallic form. Eric Bensen's mentor, who directs the project, is hinting to the scientific world that they've met the challenge. The technical articles won't be released until next month, but high-tech businesses are already fighting to get in on the profits.''

''And where there's big money there's a motive for murder even among scientists, I guess,'' Rose said.

''Right. And this is not your mother's hydrogen research. Let me show you how Eric's gas gun works.''

Rose stood up and poured more iced tea into our glasses. She'd already expressed disapproval at my meager selection of beverages. I don't drink alcohol and always forget to keep wine or beer on hand for guests. Peter, on his best behavior, claimed to prefer iced tea.

I went to my desk for a pad of paper, but by the time I returned, their eyes had glazed over. I knew I'd lost them, just as I had in our school days when I was excited about a science fair project and my friends wanted to go for pizza. I solved the problem back then by talking about levers and pulleys at the pizza parlor. *That's what I'll do now,* I thought.

''Okay,'' I said, ''let's go for pizza.''

Peter's face, dark and unwrinkled at fifty-six, took on the expression of a schoolboy caught stifling a yawn in class.

Rose threw up her hands and let out her deep throaty laugh, still marked by the telltale hoarseness of a smoker, although she'd quit years ago. ''It's Gloria's famous physics-on-the-back-of-the-napkin trick,'' she said.

It amazed me how easily the three of us fell into our old pattern of negotiating. We made a deal—we'd go out for science-free pizza, but not until I made a phone call to Sergeant Matt Gennaro at the Revere Police Department, the detective I'd worked with on the convicted chemist case. I wanted a copy of the police report on Eric Bensen's murder. And, as Rose figured, I hoped he'd ask for my help with the investigation.

"I think it's strange that the police department would hire a physicist," Peter said.

"Frank was able to set that up through his connections. It's certainly no stranger than hiring a psychic," Rose said, making me proud of her. "And Gloria has an outstanding reputation as a scientist."

"I know that," Peter said, addressing Rose. "Hasn't the *Revere Journal* been documenting her career for us? Every time Dr. Lamerino has a new publication or gets an award, they print a notice. You'd think she never left town."

"That wouldn't be because the editor is Rose and Frank's son, would it?" I asked.

"Not at all," Rose said. "It's more like 'local girl makes good.' And John is always looking for feel-good-about-Revere stories. It beats headlines like 'townies drive out newcomers.' "

"None of this explains why you need to sell yourself to the police," Peter said, finally turning to me. "If you need money—"

"It's not the money." I said, interrupting Peter before he could finish his sentence, which sounded like the beginning of an offer I'd have to refuse.

It was hard to explain, but I still didn't have quite enough to do in Revere. I'd signed up as a volunteer at the library and set up my computer to network with science consultants in the area. I also had a couple of science education contracts to finish for a museum in San Francisco, but that was a far cry from the number of projects I was used to handling at one time.

I had to admit, at least to myself, that my social life was also a factor in wanting to work on Eric's murder investigation. I'd wanted to get to know Matt Gennaro personally ever since I met him on the tungsten case, and I wasn't used to acting on such feelings without an excuse. I brushed aside the embarrassing thought that Eric Bensen's murder was designed to enrich my intellectual and my social life.

Matt was my age, a widower for ten years, and had the look of all my favorite Italian-American movie stars, including a shadowy beard that never went completely away, and dark brown eyes that looked droopy and sad until you got them smiling. I knew he owned a house on Fernwood Avenue, close to the center of the city, and I wished I could think of a safe way to determine whether he lived alone. Was it normal, I wondered, for a woman to work at a career until retirement and then consider dating? Or was it the death of my fiancé, Al Gravese, three months before our wedding that shaped my life?

It was always easy to put off answering the big questions, and with Rose and Peter waiting for me, I had a good excuse. I left a message for Matt and drove my friends in my new Cadillac to The Fenway Pizzeria, a few blocks from City Hall on Broadway, one of Revere's main streets. The evening was cool and crisp and the maples and birches wore the glorious reds and yellows that I'd missed so much during my years in California.

The Fenway had the best pizza in this neighborhood where at one time blonds and blue eyes were scarce. All of us had grown up second- or third-generation Italian. Looking at our eighth-grade class photograph you'd think all thirty or so students were related. Boys and girls alike, most of us had olive skin, dark hair, and about ten too many pounds on our short bodies. Peter was one of the exceptions, having the long, thin torso and angular features that were more characteristic of his Sicilian grandparents.

We'd all learned Italian as children and Peter had taught Italian language and literature, along with European history, at the new Revere High. He still had a full-time schedule of classes with no plans for retiring. I didn't ask why he'd never married. I figured he'd tell me soon enough.

As I looked around The Fenway, the routine meeting place after basketball games when I was in school, I half expected to see my old Revere High chums. For all I knew, these *were* my old chums. Most of the patrons on that Tuesday evening looked old enough for the class of 1958. Evidently the youth of present-day Revere hung out in a different spot. From the jukebox music that greeted us at the door—Julius La Rosa's "That's Amore"—I was able to pinpoint just where The Fenway got stuck in time.

Maybe they wanted to humor me, but once we'd ordered our extra-large combination pizza and drinks, Rose and Peter asked me to tell them about the murder victim, Eric Bensen.

"Did you know him personally?" Peter asked.

"He was in California at the Berkeley lab for about a year," I said, "to learn supercomputer programming techniques that he could apply to the equations for his hydrogen research. Two other local physicists were with him. We had mutual friends who introduced us because we're all from this area and we formed a dinner group that included Eric and his wife."

For some reason, I left out details about Eric's wife, Janice Bensen, and her incessant whining. When Janice was around, we were all embarrassed for Eric. She was tired of being poor, she'd remind us, working at a dead-end clerical job while waiting for Eric to finish his degree.

"My biological clock is ticking," Janice said often, as we tried to enjoy world-class Berkeley and San Francisco seafood restaurants. "I don't see why we can't move back to Revere and be near our families."

In spite of my agreement with Rose and Peter, I made another attempt to explain what was so different about the hydrogen experiments Eric had worked on. After all, they did ask what I knew about Eric. This time they were more patient. Maybe it was the yeasty smell of thick-crust pizza dough and the promise of mushrooms, anchovies, and extra cheese, plus Michelob on tap. I noticed Peter didn't order iced tea.

I spread a napkin on the scratched red Formica tabletop and

drew a long narrow rectangle, working around the little map of Italy in the corner and being careful not to tear the thin paper. I added a pointed section to one end of the rectangle, and a placed a round target next to it.

''Just like a regular gun and target,'' I said, my fingers working to add detail to the drawing. ''Except in this case the gun is a sixty-foot-long compression chamber and the target is liquid hydrogen. After a buildup of pressure, the shock wave from the gun is enough to turn the hydrogen target into a metal.''

I sketched in a piston, and some arrows to show the direction of the shock waves, then sat back, admiring my art, once again filled with awe at the wonders of technology.

''For a fraction of a second the hydrogen becomes metallic and conducts electricity with almost no resistance—superconductivity. Very exciting.''

Apparently my companions didn't experience this exhilaration. Our waitress, who also looked like a member of the class of 1958, had delivered our pizza and Peter was forcing the slices into neat triangles and arranging them on The Fenway's heavy white plates.

''A fraction of a second,'' Rose said, her voice rising above Julius La Rosa's. ''That's worth making a fuss over?''

''I still don't get how it could be connected to a murder,'' Peter said.

I already had a theory about that, but I wasn't sure I wanted to share it. My theory involved thinking bad things about physicists, something I was always reluctant to do. There were shrines in my heart to Galileo, Isaac Newton, and Marie Curie. I didn't want to clutter my mind with anything that implied that scientists of today were less than perfect.

I finally decided that Rose and Peter could be trusted, and besides, I needed to get my thoughts out in the open so I could analyze them better. I rationalized that the noise from the jukebox would shield our conversation from the general public that crowded the pizza parlor.

''There's a lot of money involved,'' I said, ''as well as

careers, fortunes, and reputations on the line. Just before he left California to come back here, Eric hinted that there might be something wrong with the data his team submitted to an important journal. I know his mentor and colleagues were upset that Eric wanted to look into some discrepancy before they published their data.''

As I talked, an image of the evening came back to me—Eric getting our attention with loud talk about data tampering, deception, and fraud. We were at a Saint Patrick's Day party thrown by one of his colleagues, Jim Guffy, and I had a vague memory of Eric's mentor, Ralph Leder, rushing to Eric's side and ushering him out of the room.

``I thought scientists were supposed to be objective and above all that,'' Rose said. ``Are you sure you're not talking about lawyers?'' From Rose, the mother-in-law of two lawyers, whom she loved, this comment had a lighthearted ring.

``What happened to our science-free pizza?'' Peter asked, pulling crumbs from his jacket and placing them in a neat pile on his plate. ``Tell us about your life in California.''

As hard as I tried, I couldn't keep the conversation on safe science instead of drifting to more personal matters. Peter was pushing hard, and not just with his long legs that I kept bumping into under The Fenway's table.

``Why did you run away and stay away all these years, Gloria?'' he asked.

``I don't think of it as running away. I went to the West Coast to study physics.''

``As if there aren't places to study physics in Boston.''

``I needed a change.''

``Well, that's called running away.''

``If that's how you see it. I don't,'' I said, hoping my voice carried more conviction than I felt. Whether I'd run away or not was one of the questions I'd come back to answer, but not in this environment, and not at Peter's will.

Rose was twisting her napkin, her eyes darting from me to Peter as if she were a spectator at a tense volleyball game. I knew she could tell I was not having a good time. Rose had eaten only one slice of pizza, while I'd had three and contemplated a fourth as I became more and more uncomfortable with Peter's inquisition. Another clue about why there was such a huge difference in weight between me and Rose.

After a couple of more rounds of questions without answers—Why had I sneaked back to see my father when he was dying and not contacted anyone except Rose and Frank, who buried him? Why did I finally leave California and come "home"? Was I back for good?—I was happy to see our venerable waitress hovering over us with a pitcher of dark beer in one hand and our check in the other, using her penciled-in eyebrows to ask which we wanted.

With a passing glance at the crumbs on our dented tray and a quick check of the plates in front of Rose and Peter, I said, "We'll take the tab."

I looked across the table at Peter, saw the surprised look on his face, and realized that feminism had left him behind. I was sure that the last time I had pizza with him, he called the shots and paid the bill. Probably even held my coat for me. I was beginning to think that two or three hours with Peter every thirty years was enough.

"My treat," I said, pulling my wallet out of my purse.

Chapter Three

Anxious to get back to my apartment and check my answering machine for a message from Sgt. Matt Gennaro, I managed to leave no doubt about my lack of interest in nightcaps. I dropped my friends at the curb and suggested that Peter drive Rose to her home across town.

"I'm beat," I said, with as loud a sigh as I could muster after three-and-a-half slices of pizza. Rose had weighed in at one-and-a-half slices.

Peter frowned as he climbed out of my spacious back seat, then leaned into my window and gave me a kiss, something halfway between the friend and the lover varieties. I found myself leaning toward the friend variety and responded accordingly. It hadn't taken me long to remember why we'd broken up in the first place.

"I'll call you, Gloria," Peter said. "It's not going to be another thirty years."

I smiled and let him have the last word for the moment.

I pulled in to the enormous mortuary garage, parked my car next to one of the Galigani hearses, and headed up the inside stairs to my apartment, passing the main funeral parlor on the first floor. Although there was no body laid out that evening, the air was heavy with leftover flower smells. I'd have sworn that I also smelled formaldehyde and Silktex, Frank's standard anticoagulant, but he said it was my imagination.

"The prep room is very well ventilated, following O.S.H.A. standards," Frank had assured me. "And we use the latest in low-fuming chemicals."

A graduate of the New England Institute of Mortuary Science, Frank was as proud as any scientist would be of his policy of keeping up with the changing technology in his field. Although he had outside assistants and had successfully groomed his firstborn son, Robert, to follow in his footsteps, Frank participated in every aspect of his undertaking business, from comforting bereaved families to performing an occasional embalming.

Even empty, funeral parlor rooms always seemed quieter to me than other spaces, as if the dead were able to absorb all natural background noise. Galigani's was on a busy side street, but once inside, it felt like what I imagined the interior of a vacuum tube to be like.

The second-floor offices of Galigani's, at the top of a beautiful old stairway with a mahogany banister, were visible from the street-level foyer. Arranged symmetrically around the landing were two rooms where Rose and her assistant Martha worked during the day, in charge of correspondence, bookkeeping, and general management of the business. Frank had a smaller first-floor office between the main parlor and the casket showroom.

My apartment was on the third floor, a one-bedroom flat, with a small kitchen and good-sized living room, originally meant for a resident caretaker in the days before alarm systems. Except for two matching pale blue glide rockers, I'd given my furniture to a battered women's shelter in Berkeley, and started over in Revere with a few new pieces of modern design, in grays and blues to match the rockers.

Above me at Galigani's was an attic where Rose and Frank had been storing some of my belongings for the last thirty years. I'd planned to make regular trips up there to sort through my cartons, but hadn't made much headway in four months.

Entering my apartment, I went immediately to the answering machine and pushed the button. Unlike Peter, I had all the conveniences of twentieth-century technology that I could afford, from a top-of-the-line computer system and cordless phone to an electronic Rolodex file that I carried in my purse.

Matt Gennaro's hoped-for message was there and I smiled as I listened to his low, scratchy voice.

"I was just about to call you," he said. "I'd like to talk about the possibility of having your help with a new investigation. I'm wondering if you'll be able to meet me for lunch tomorrow. Say, Russo's on Broadway at twelve-thirty. I'll look for you there unless I hear otherwise."

"Yes," I said out loud to my empty rooms, tossing my head back like a rookie cop snapping to attention.

Two for one, I thought. *A job and a date.* I decided to wait until morning to call the police department. I knew from my previous experience working with him that Matt Gennaro's regular routine was to have a breakfast of black coffee and a bagel at his desk at about eight o'clock, his "form-filling-out time," he called it.

It was the first time since hearing about Eric Bensen's death that I was alone and able to absorb the fact that someone I knew had been murdered. I looked out my window, amazed at the calmness of the October evening, although I'd been out in it only a few minutes earlier. I looked carefully into the dark night and wouldn't have been surprised if a bolt of lightning shot across the cloudless sky to denounce the unnatural event that had taken place on Charger Street.

I put on a CD of piano music and settled in one of my rockers with the newspaper, a notebook, and pencil, but before I looked at them I rocked back and forth, letting Mozart's sonatas calm my mind. Although we hadn't been close, Eric was a friend and a colleague at the beginning of a promising career, and I hated the idea that he'd been the victim of violence.

I opened the newspaper and read the brief account. A clear case of murder, according to the police. The victim was a thirty-one-year-old physics graduate student, the reporter noted. Three shots had been fired from a distance into his chest, sometime between midnight and four in the morning on Tuesday, October eleventh. He was found by a security guard in his lab at the northern edge of Revere on Charger Street, in a building that was an off-campus annex to the Physics Department of Massachusetts University. No sign of struggle. Nothing missing as far as anyone could tell. The lab had a great deal of expensive equipment, the article said, but nothing very portable or valuable for trading on the street. Physics Department officials hadn't had a chance to examine the room closely to see if small items were missing.

I checked the digital clock on my desk. Nine forty-five P.M.; six forty-five in California. I usually talked to my good friend Elaine Cody on weekends, but I knew she'd want to hear about Eric's murder as soon as possible. I punched in her Berkeley phone number and reached her immediately.

"Gloria," she said. "I was just going to call you. What happened to Eric Bensen? I heard just the briefest snippet on my car radio driving home."

I told Elaine all I knew about the murder and offered to make arrangements for flowers for Eric. Across the miles I pictured Elaine in a pleated skirt, sweater set, and pearls. With her classic preppy wardrobe and shoulder-length hair, blond in her youth, Elaine had earned the nickname "Radcliffe." Unlike most Californians, she always dressed up for her work as a technical writer at our lab.

"I don't believe in clothes that have no buttons or zippers," she'd say as we observed the parade of lab employees arriving for work in sweat suits in the winter and cutoffs and T-shirts in the summer.

"Are you going to work on the murder case?" Elaine asked.

"I don't know yet. I hope so."

"Be careful, Gloria."

I laughed at the thought that there might be danger connected to my police work.

"I'm only a consultant," I said. "I work with pencil and paper, no guns or gangs."

"Still," Elaine said. "Be careful. When are you coming out? You said after the summer."

"Maybe before Christmas."

"I miss you."

"I miss you, too."

We hung up, both knowing that I had no intention of going to the West Coast before the holidays. I felt I needed at least one stable year in my new home to determine which coast I wanted to spend the next thirty years on. Elaine had visited me in Revere, the first of the rash of visitors I'd had during my first two months back. As I took my California friends to Boston's fine museums and for walks around the Freedom Trail, I felt like a tourist myself, a feeling I was trying to get over. Every time I went to Logan Airport to pick up or deliver a guest, I wondered if I was the one who should be getting on the plane. Invariably during my weekly phone conversations with Elaine, she told me about a wedding or birthday party that I wished I could have attended—very distracting in terms of my ability to feel like a New England native again.

"If you got through the hot sticky summer, you're a native," Rose had told me on Labor Day, not without self-interest.

Although I knew I was in a minority, for me, the gray humid air was a welcome relief from the stark sunlight of California that required polarizing lenses nearly every day of the year.

I called a few other people in Berkeley who knew Eric at least as well as I did, and collected names for flowers. Then I slid my notepad on top of the folded newspaper and started to organize my thoughts in anticipation of another go at detective work.

Eric's mentor, Dr. Ralph Leder, was much older than Eric, probably in his late fifties, I thought. I'd met him only three or four times when he visited Eric in California. He was a tall, broad-shouldered midwesterner, with thick blond and gray hair and a large square face, his slow movements in sharp contrast to his quick mind. He was well-published and respected, but he'd made it obvious that he was counting on the gas gun experiments for further recognition in his field. I remembered a talk Leder gave to our group in California in the spring, following the news releases in the popular press. His ambitions filled the overhead screen in the large conference room:

Our work in metallic hydrogen will:

- Push the envelope in understanding the composition of Jupiter
- Secure our place in the development of superconductivity for commercial use
- Put us out front in the transfer of technology to American industry

He'd left off "bring us fame and fortune," but the message was clear. I couldn't help thinking that with so much money at stake, if Leder thought Eric was going to expose any shady activities on the part of the research team, he might be unhappy enough to kill him. I put four stars next to Leder's name, my equivalent of "most likely suspect."

Besides Leder, Eric, and six authors who were permanent residents of California, two other Revere-based physicists worked on the journal article that was to catapult the hydrogen research team to award-winning status—Connie Provenza and Jim Guffy, post-docs who were stretching their funds and their dissertation research into one more year after receiving their doctoral degrees. Like Eric, they'd spent most of the year in California and had been back in the Boston area slightly longer than I had, arriving sometime in late May.

Connie Provenza had just turned thirty and lived in Chelsea, a city bordering Revere on the south, with her boyfriend Bill Gordon, a third-year law student at Boston's Northeastern University. Connie, the main theorist in the group, seemed to me very ambitious, often talking about breaking through the glass ceiling. Her announced plans were to capitalize on the success of the hydrogen experiments, get a quick MBA, and head for corporate America. She was bright and attractive, and one of the main difficulties of her present life seemed to be warding off the advances of Ralph Leder, who was also her mentor.

In deference to her gender, which she would not like, I gave Connie only three stars, for ''possible suspect.''

Jim Guffy was a little younger than Connie, an Irish-American Catholic, unmarried, and as conservative as if he'd never heard of Pope John XXIII and the reforms of Vatican II. I remembered heated debates about the old and new Catholic Mass, and the Church's unchanging position on sexual morality and the role of women. Jim's contribution to the research team was his skill as an experimentalist. Thoroughly involved with the hardware, Jim could kludge together a high-voltage power supply or a digital temperature probe in a matter of hours.

Thinking about Jim's moral high ground and daily mass, I gave him no stars, for ''unlikely suspect.''

Both Connie and Jim were among the people in our occasional dinner group. Each month we'd explore a different San Francisco fish emporium or a new ethnic menu, which Berkeley offered on almost every street corner—Thai, Afghan, Iranian, to name a few, plus cuisine from places that had been countries for only a month or so.

Not that anyone was asking, but I decided I could rule out the six California scientists, once I verified that they were still on the West Coast. *Brilliant,* I told myself. *If this is the best I can do, I'd better go to bed.*

Just after I turned out my reading lamp, I heard the now-familiar noise of the garage door opening, two floors below my bedroom. I stretched across the bed to look out the window. Through my parted white linen drapes, I saw a Galigani hearse leave the driveway and pull out onto Tuttle Street. The long black vehicle moved slowly across the gray shadows cast by the streetlight, and for a moment I thought I'd tuned in to a classic movie channel.

At the same time, my phone rang and Rose's voice came over the line.

"I don't want to freak you out," she said. "But it turns out Eric Bensen is going to be waked at our place—your place."

I tried not to register too much dismay, although this would be a first for me. Usually I didn't know the corpses laid out in my building.

"Isn't Cavallo's closer to where the Bensens live?" I asked, trying not to sound like I was rooting for the competition.

"Not at all. They're way over by the Chelsea overpass, remember? And anyway, Eric's grandmother lives in the senior apartments across from St. Anthony's, right down the street, so they signed on with us. Does that bother you?"

"No, it's just different," I said, still looking out the window. I was aware of the new housing for the elderly that Rose was talking about. Almost nightly I heard ambulances and police vehicles screaming past my apartment on their way to the facility.

"One of the hearses will be leaving soon to pick up the body," Rose said, not having the advantage I did of seeing the hearse already turning the corner onto Revere Street. "It didn't take them very long at the morgue. I guess the cause of death was cut-and-dried. Frank's going to work on Eric himself and he'll be ready at the end of the week, probably Friday evening."

I'd learned a lot more than I cared to about how Frank "worked on" his clients. When I first moved in, Frank gave me a tour, taking me down in the rickety old elevator used to transport the bodies between the floors. Most unforgettable was the prep room where Frank and his staff, headed by his older son Robert, did the embalming. The shiny facility, looking as clean as an operating room, which in a sense it was, was at the back of the building, in the basement. Often when I was home during the day I'd hear the sound of the pumping machines. Thanks to Frank's excellent presentation, I could envision pint after pint of human blood being drained from a body and replaced with embalming fluids.

The washer and dryer were also in the basement, and so far I had managed to arrange my laundry chores so they coincided with a lack of activity in the prep room.

I dropped the drapes as the taillights of the Galigani hearse disappeared around a bend in the street.

"Thanks for telling me," I said to Rose. "By the way, you didn't seem surprised to find Peter here tonight."

"He told me not to warn you. I knew he was going to drop in on you unannounced, but not necessarily tonight. I hope I didn't spoil a twosome."

"I'm very glad you did."

"I gathered as much," Rose said, with a laugh. "Thanks to your bickering I ate more than I needed to."

"Really? I didn't."

"Have you heard from your detective?"

"Yes. I'm going to have lunch with him tomorrow."

I expected something like "aha" from Rose, and wasn't disappointed.

"Yeah," she said. "Let's invite him—"

"No," I said, interrupting her. "It's just business."

"We'll see," Rose said as we hung up, making me regret telling her about lunch. Ever since I'd been back, Rose's pace in the matter of my personal life had more acceleration than I was comfortable with. She'd dragged out every unattached man over fifty that she knew in an attempt to make me part of a pair. She was also after me to "do something about my appearance," telling me she saw more makeup on the nuns who taught catechism at St. Anthony's.

"And just a little rinse to soften the gray," she'd say to me, reaching for the wiry curls around my face.

"I love you dearly," I'd tell her. "I envy your figure and your family, but not your auburn highlights."

I settled back in my bed, feeling very fortunate to have a friend to talk to that way. As I drifted off to sleep, three questions paraded in front of my brain—was Eric Bensen's body going to be worked on that night in the prep room? Should his wife Janice be on my suspect list? And what should I wear to lunch with Matt Gennaro?

I couldn't quite remember if we were still at the Doctor-Sergeant stage or if we'd gotten as far as Gloria and Matt.

Chapter Four

I woke up to Columbus Day, October twelfth.

Besides the changing seasons, another thing about the East Coast that I'd missed were holidays like Patriots' Day on the third Monday in April and Bunker Hill Day on June seventeenth. Berkeley parking meters called October twelfth Indigenous Peoples Day, and California residents in general emphasized a different set of holidays, like Mexican Independence Day on May fifth, and Admission Day on September ninth.

"Is that some holiday for school registration?" I'd asked when I was new on the West Coast. My greatly amused friends informed me that the holiday was to commemorate California's admission into the union.

To recover some dignity, I reminded them that I was from Massachusetts, one of the states that was on the admissions committee.

"You ought to thank me," I'd said, and we called a truce.

I looked at my wardrobe choices. I have clothes in at least two sizes, one set for my thinner times in size twelve and the other, more often used, in size fourteen. My resolution to get to a ten by fall hadn't worked out so I put on my mid-range dark gray suit and a white cotton shell. I added a necklace of hematite beads and pinned a small replica of crossed Italian and American flags to my lapel.

Just as when I was a kid, there'd be a parade later in the day starting at the base of the statue of Christopher Columbus outside St. Anthony's Church and flowing down Revere Street to the beach. I remembered years long past, watching my father march with the Sons of Italy, carrying the huge bass drum around his strong dark neck. I wondered if they kept the custom of ending up back at the church with a special mass at its main altar. No wonder we used to think Columbus was one of the saints.

I checked the clock. For two reasons, I wanted to arrive early at Russo's Café where I was to meet Matt. The first reason was tied to another inherited trait from my mother. Josephine would have the table set for dinner—she called it supper—by four in the afternoon. If you were ten minutes late, she'd be furious. She'd have been waiting two hours and ten minutes by then, and blamed you for every second.

''Why did you even bother to come?'' she'd ask, blowing smoke through her nose and breathing heavily under her flowered cotton apron.

I was a little better than that since my lifestyle didn't permit all-day meal preparation, but still, I had a reputation among my friends for always being way ahead of schedule.

The second reason I wanted to be early was that I was resisting the image of Matt and the rest of Russo's lunch crowd seeing me pull up in my sleek Cadillac. I didn't want people to think I was running for office. I began to doubt the wisdom of my deal with the Galiganis.

''You'll get used to it,'' Rose had told me. Small comfort, since it came from someone who thought of six-cylinder cars as toys for teenagers.

Russo's Café, an upscale sandwich and coffee shop a block from the post office on Broadway, was at the site of the old five-and-ten where I bought all my Christmas presents until I was in college. The new owners had taken advantage of the large room and high ornate ceiling to create the look of old Rome, with plaster columns and murals of chariots and ancient fountains. Several armless white sculpted figures were scattered among the small round tables, as if waiting to be fed.

Although I'd arrived early enough to park in one of the few spots around the back of the restaurant, Matt was already at a table with an espresso and a stack of papers and manila folders in front of him. As I approached, I could tell he didn't know whether or not to stand. Feminism confuses a lot of men, I remembered. He rose halfway and rearranged the table so that the piles of paper were out of the way of the second place setting. *Smooth move,* I thought.

I guessed that Matt also had two wardrobes. He was a little thick around the middle, but not fat, just enough to give him a solid appearance. His hair had about the same amount of gray as mine, still showing up dark in photographs, but mostly gray as it fell on the hairdresser's cloth. His long nose, with its straight downward slope, was also like mine and fit right in with the Mediterranean décor. As I considered the similarities in our appearances, I wondered if I was infatuated with my twin. I remembered reading a pop psychology article that said it was a sign of high self-esteem if you were attracted to people who look like you. I decided not to pursue that concept, conscious that a little psychological knowledge is a dangerous thing.

The second awkward moment after the should-I-stand-for-a-lady dilemma consisted of a round of call-me-Matt, call-me-Gloria. We eased the situation by getting down to business.

"Here's the report," Matt said, his voice as gravelly as I had remembered. "Not much to go on, but since you know a lot of the principals, you might have some ideas."

I settled down to the six pages of single-spaced type and a sheaf of crime scene photographs while Matt excused himself. I watched him walk past the kitchen to the men's room, his dark rumpled suit receding into a row of fake Italian palms. I wondered what percent of my excitement was from seeing him again and what percent from the challenging puzzle before me. I'd long ago accepted the occupational hazard of a lifelong career in science—trying to measure everything. Even excitement.

I opened the envelope of photographs, keeping it low on my lap so as not to offend the sensibilities of those dining at tables around me. Most of the other patrons at Russo's were in business suits and career dresses and I envisioned them as tax accountants and retail clerks and at other non-bloody occupations.

I noted with relief that these crime scene photographs were a little easier to take than the ones I'd had to look at for my first case, which were of a gruesome murder in a chemistry lab. Eric Bensen was the victim of a relatively clean murder. I found it easier to take the pools of blood around his torso, as long as all of his body parts were intact. I saw that Eric had fallen on his side, and looked almost comfortable spread out on his lab floor. The fabric of his khaki pants that was visible looked clean, and his left arm was tucked under his upper body as if he were taking a quick nap on a small red carpet.

I took a deep breath and a long drink of lemony water to counteract the queasiness that had come to my stomach in spite of the tidiness of the crime scene, and moved on to read the pages of text. I was ready with some questions when Matt returned.

''There's nothing in this report about disks or printout around Eric's desk,'' I said. ''His computer screen is blank and the area around him looks bare in these photographs. Would the officers have listed papers and disks if they were there?''

''Absolutely,'' Matt said. ''Maybe he was doing something else that didn't require the computer?''

I thought about this as our waiter brought my dry cappuccino and eggplant and pepper sandwiches for both of us.

I pulled out the photograph with the best shot of Eric's workplace. His computer monitor and keyboard were surrounded by yellow sticky notes and dozens of small figures, a few of which I could identify—Batman, Spider-Man, Wonder Woman, Superman. Among the other action heroes in different sizes was a small white plaster bust of Albert Einstein, similar to ones I'd seen in science museum gift shops. I could also make out a soft drink can, a framed photograph of his wife, Janice, and a mug full of pens and pencils, but there was no sign of floppies or hard copy anywhere.

As I pointed to the peripheral equipment in the photograph, Matt pulled out a pair of rimless half glasses and followed my fingers with his gaze.

"This shows Eric had a complete system with his own printer and drives," I said, "so he wasn't just using a terminal connected to a mainframe. It's hard to believe all his disks and printout are stored out of sight."

"So, does that mean you think the murderer stole the computer stuff?" Matt asked. "And if so, why?"

While we ate, I told Matt my initial theory that the murderer might be a scientist who stood to lose a lot if Eric retracted the journal article with their hydrogen data.

"Then it would make sense that the killer would try to remove all evidence that there was something wrong with their work," I said. "And that evidence would most likely have been around Eric's computer."

"Wouldn't the error in the data eventually be found out anyway?" Matt asked.

Temporarily abandoning loyalty to my profession, I explained that this kind of thing happened all the time. Not murders necessarily, but borderline dishonesty. It wouldn't be the first time scientists exaggerated the potential of a new technology in order to get funding to further the research.

Although I still didn't know the exact nature of the discrepancy or error Eric had uncovered, I'd been around research science long enough to make a good guess. I told Matt that the error wasn't necessarily an incorrect number or calculation. It could be that the team had neglected to account for some particular factor in their experiment, like a magnetic effect, or a temperature dependency. In an extreme case, scientists who used complicated computer programs to do their calculations could actually fake data, by adding a line or two to their software that even another expert in the field might not be able to uncover.

"Maybe a few years later," I told Matt, "the discrepancy

between promise and fulfillment would be obvious, but it could be suppressed until long after money had been granted and large facilities were built. And even then, it could be passed off as something no one could have known before.''

''Hmph,'' was all I heard from Matt, so I continued.

Reluctantly, I gave him some other examples of this kind of incident, drawing from the history of weapons technology and nuclear energy.

Matt had been taking notes with his right hand, holding his sandwich in his left. He put down both, wiped his hands on his napkin, and shook his head, as if he'd just heard about another pop idol on drugs.

''I guess I'm still naive about what goes on in the world of science,'' he said. ''I feel a lot more comfortable with people killing each other over insurance money or large family fortunes. I understand the motives involved in wills or domestic situations, but I'm out of my league here.''

The phrase ''domestic situations'' got my attention and I wondered if I should I tell Matt about Janice. Not now, I decided. As bitter as Janice Bensen seemed to be about her life with Eric, I couldn't picture her standing in front of him with a gun and shooting three times. But then, I was new to this life of crime-solving, so it was hard to picture anyone other than an obvious madman killing another person.

Awkward moment number three came when our waiter brought the check. I reached for my purse. Matt smiled and held up his hand like a stop signal.

''Department expense,'' he said.

Another smooth move. Like my late beloved Uncle Tony, Matt had a left-leaning grin and a habit of raising his thick eyebrows when he smiled. I mentally gave Matt a role in the fourth Godfather movie, which I desperately hoped was in the works. I cast him as head of security in a legitimate family pastry business.

''I wonder if you'd consider visiting the murder scene with me,'' Matt asked, leaning forward to stuff his wallet in his back pocket. His jacket fell open just enough for me to see the gun holstered in a light brown leather case under his arm.

It was hard to play it cool, but I managed a simple, "I'd be happy to."

"I brought this along in case you agreed," Matt said, spreading a legal-sized packet of paper in front of me. Another charming crooked smile.

I recognized the standard consultant's contract, like the one I'd signed a few months before in Matt's office. Matt reminded me of the conditions of the contract. I wasn't an investigator in the sense that he was, so I couldn't ask suspects about alibis, for instance, or motive. But I could be present when he asked those questions, and I could ask technical questions, like how close was this research to achieving full superconductivity at room temperatures.

He also warned me, as he did the last time, not to do any personal interviews on my own.

"At this point, everyone who knew Eric Bensen and had a motive and the opportunity to kill him is a suspect," Matt said. "And we don't want you in any danger."

Matt had no reason to think I'd do any sleuthing on the side. On my last contract, I'd stuck to the rules, and done only what was required of me. Moreover, I'd never been one to take risks when it came to my body or any of its parts. I wouldn't even consent to let Rose's hairdresser have a go at getting rid of my gray hair. I was afraid she'd do just that, and I'd be bald.

"I have no plans to play detective," I said, breaking into what I hoped was delightful, flattering laughter.

But this case felt different to me from my one and only other murder case. I'd known Eric Bensen and all the more obvious suspects personally, and I wondered if I meant what I said.

Chapter Five

As much as I'd looked forward to going to the Columbus Day parade, I agreed with Matt that we needed to get to the gas gun lab right away. I left my Cadillac and rode with him in his unmarked beige Ford. He drove to within a block of the parade, so at least I heard the band music, smelled the popcorn, and felt a little vibration from the pounding of hundreds of boots hitting the pavement at the same time.

"I could use my light and siren and plow through the lines—get you really close to the action," Matt offered.

"I don't think so," I said, afraid he was serious.

We headed across town just after one o'clock, driving through older residential sections of Revere that hadn't changed much over the years, with small shingled houses and well-kept lawns, tiny by the standards of the newer developments in the western part of the city. Most of these side streets off Broadway still held enough tall elms and maples to give the city the look of a fall scene on a postcard.

Matt wanted one more look around Eric's cubicle before our scheduled meeting with Dr. Ralph Leder, the project leader for the hydrogen research. We entered the building, made our way to the basement, and walked toward the steep ramp that led down another half level to the gas gun lab. The crime scene tape was still hanging across the ramp and a uniformed policewoman was sitting on a chair in the corridor. I remembered reading in the police report that the security guard had found Eric's body at four in the morning when he noticed that the ramp door was open.

"Pretty quiet down here," the policewoman said as Matt greeted her and unlocked the door. Since she made no attempt to cover a wide yawn, I figured she knew Matt from the station. Some parts of police work are more interesting than others, I thought, happy to be involved in a new puzzle.

The temperature seemed to drop two degrees with each foot as Matt and I made our way down, putting this sub-basement at about forty-five degrees, colder than the air outside. I breathed in the odor of rust and cold metal and realized I missed walking around in places like this. I missed the thick log book that I carried around all day and my short white cotton coat, its pockets cluttered with scraps of paper and small tools.

The gas gun lab was one enormous room, divided into sections by a motley selection of drab green felt partitions and black plastic curtains. To a layperson the multimillion-dollar sixty-foot gas gun at the far end of the room would be hard to distinguish from the water pipes that lined the ceiling. Tiny red and green lights from the row of high-voltage power supplies called attention to the giant piece of equipment resting on brackets above them.

The rest of the room in front of the gas gun, uncarpeted and unpainted, held cubicles with desks and workbenches. There were no windows and just the one door that led to the ramp and then to the basement corridor. Even with all the overhead lights on, the room looked overcast, as if it might rain any minute. It was easy to understand how someone could have entered and left this isolated area unnoticed.

Matt took me over to Eric's desk, a few yards in from the edge of the ramp door, his chair facing the entrance. I remembered that the newspaper account said the shots were fired from a distance and I asked Matt about it, since there wasn't what I considered a great distance between Eric's chair and the door.

"A distance means more than a foot," Matt said, and although he was anything but patronizing, I felt like the novice I was. I made a resolution to check the World Wide Web for police procedural information before I asked any more stupid questions.

I stepped onto the plastic pad under Eric's chair for a closer look at his computer system.

''Has anyone tried to pull up the last file Eric was working on?'' I asked.

''We did boot up the machine, but there wasn't anything listed with a time for late Monday night or early Tuesday morning.''

I told Matt that Eric was the computer genius of the project, and that all of his responsibilities revolved around the software he was writing. I couldn't imagine that he'd come here in the middle of the night to do anything but computer work.

''I think it would be worthwhile to dig deeper and see if a file was deleted by the murderer,'' I said.

''If it's deleted, it's gone, right?''

''Not exactly. If you just hit 'delete,' the name of the file will disappear from the directory and you won't see it listed anymore, but the file's still in there somewhere, and there's software available that will allow you to retrieve it.''

''I never knew that,'' Matt said. ''Let's hope the killer didn't either. I'll ask Casey over at our computer lab to come by and check it out.''

As we turned to leave, I looked at Eric's computer monitor. His collection of action figures was there, but something about them looked different from what I remembered seeing in the police photographs.

I made a note to look again at the photographs, which we'd left in Matt's car.

As a small gesture toward health and fitness, we took the stairs to the second floor. Leder was standing outside his office talking to a young woman with the efficient look of a secretary. He looked past her and walked over to greet us with a wide smile.

Leder took my hand and gave it a couple of light pats.

''How unfortunate to meet again under these circumstances,'' he said. He spoke in low tones, looking down from his six-foot height at me and Matt. I noticed how closely his gold-toned turtleneck matched the part of his hair that wasn't gray.

To Matt he said, "I hope you're here to tell me that we can have our lab back."

"We're as anxious for that as you are, sir," Matt answered. "In a couple of days, I hope. First, I'd like to know more about the project Eric was working on. Dr. Lamerino's along so she can translate for me when we get back to the station."

Matt smiled at me when he came to the last sentence and I felt a tiny, but distinctive, twinge in my chest.

"Oh, Gloria and I are old friends," Leder said. "Very bright lady. But surely you don't think Eric's murder had something to do with his work?"

"We can't rule anything out," Matt said. "Do you have information about another motive, one that doesn't involve his work?"

"No, no, but none of us are angels, you know, and Eric did have some problems that could get a man in trouble." At this, Leder winked, as if we all knew what he meant.

"Can you explain what you mean?" Matt said, his voice calm and casual, as if he'd done this before.

"Well, I don't like to gossip, especially when someone is dead, but I think Gloria here will verify that Eric's wife Janice was unhappy in her marriage and his girlfriend was tired of sneaking around. His girlfriend on this coast, that is."

Matt and I sat up straighter at the hint of a girlfriend on each coast. By this time we were all seated in Leder's office, which was furnished in the typical academic style of leftover furniture and an abundance of posters covering up an old paint job. The woman from the corridor came in with Styrofoam cups and a pot of coffee. The woman smelled of vanilla musk; the coffee smelled old and burnt.

"Yes, Eric had quite a thing going on the side," Leder said, "with our little technician, Andrea Cabrini. And this other little gal in Berkeley. I thought you'd have found out by now.'' Leder rocked back and forth in his chair with his hands behind his head.

''Did you tell this to the officer who took your statement?'' Matt asked.

''No, he was more interested in me,'' Leder said. ''Where I was—in bed with my wife, by the way—how long I've known Eric, and so on.''

Seeing Matt write *Andrea Cabrini* in his notebook, I assumed he was going to pursue this line of questioning. Instead he brought up the subject he'd come to discuss.

''Tell us about the work Eric was doing for you. You were directing his research for his degree?''

''That's correct. Eric did all the programming for fluid molecular hydrogen at over one hundred and forty gigapascals. I should also remind you that this work represents a condensed-matter physics breakthrough and gives us insight into the nature of Jupiter.''

Great, I thought, *just the kind of talk that gives physicists a bad name, pouring out jargon on a layperson as a way of gaining the upper hand.* It was time for me to speak up.

''Jupiter's ninety percent hydrogen, isn't it?'' I said. ''So whatever you find out about hydrogen will add to our knowledge of Jupiter and the rest of the solar system.''

Leder nodded and pointed high up on the wall behind him at a large poster of our sun and planets, but before he could speak again I pushed on.

''But that's not where the profits will be, is it?'' I asked.

Leder dropped his arm. His smile disappeared into the folds of skin around his lower jaw.

''Didn't I read about some preliminary talks you've had with SuperCon Tech? I think I saw something about their interest in funding the next version of the gas gun based on the results you have so far.''

Matt looked at me, then down at his notebook where he'd been doodling. I saw the symbol for infinity. Or maybe it was just a figure eight.

Leder sat forward and folded his hands on his desk blotter. His large flat forehead had the markings of a frown.

"It's not at all uncommon to form partnerships between science and industry. You should know that, Gloria," he said, as if he were explaining fractions to a dull child.

"I was just surprised to read about negotiations so soon. Wasn't it only in March that Eric was mentioning a significant problem with the data? Something about not making enough runs with the signal from the new trigger pin?"

I was guessing about the trigger pin—the device that produces an electrical signal when a shock wave hits it—but it seemed good enough to get his attention.

There's always something that strains the relationship be tween computational physicists like Eric and project directors like Leder. The physicists who work out the long, complicated equations for big projects want to keep going over every possible decimal place for accuracy. The ones who become project directors like Ralph Leder, while not entirely unscrupulous, tend to focus on the bottom line. They're looking for reportable, fundable results as quickly as possible.

"I remember that occasion," Leder said. "It was at Jim Guffy's Saint Patrick's Day party. I think we'd all agree Eric had too much to drink that night."

I noticed he didn't correct me on the trigger signal, which meant either the problem *was* with the data from the trigger signal, or Leder wasn't about to give me any free information.

"Did you pursue this problem that Eric had with your data?" Matt asked. He'd added a string of infinities to the margin of his notepad.

"As a matter of fact, I did discuss it with the team, and we came to the conclusion that our findings are solid," Leder said, looking at his watch at the same time. "Now if you'll excuse me, I have a faculty meeting in ten minutes."

Matt closed his notebook and we all stood up.

"It certainly was a pleasure seeing you again, Gloria," Leder said. His smile came back too easily, reminding me of why I distrusted him and why I'd given him four stars on my potential killer scale.

Back in Matt's car, we talked about the interview.

''What's a gigapascal?'' he asked.

''It's a unit to measure pressure. We used to refer to 'pounds per square inch' or 'psi,' which you're probably familiar with. Now we have 'pascals,' named after the French scientist. A gigapascal is a unit representing one billion pascals.''

''Is that the same Pascal who was a philosopher?''

''The same,'' I said. ''He turned to religion and philosophy at the end of his life—first he worked in mathematics and science. He published a book on geometry when he was only sixteen.''

''And you know all this?''

''I spent a lot of time in school. You pick things up if you hang around enough.''

''Right,'' Matt said, sounding like he didn't accept my explanation, which I firmly believed—if you show up at school often enough, you'll learn a lot and people will think you're smart.

''Woody Allen says eighty-eight percent of life is showing up,'' I said, to support my position.

''Is that right?''

''Well, some number like that. I saw it on a bumper sticker.''

I figured that would show him that I had a wide repertoire of resources. It did at least get a laugh.

''However you did it, nice work in there with Leder,'' he said.

In my younger days, I would have downplayed my little contribution even more, but I'd made some progress in recent years accepting myself as an intelligent and worthwhile person. To do this, I had to keep tuning out Josephine's early programming that I was lazy and would never amount to anything. She died before I knew how to correct that impression.

I finally accepted Matt's compliment graciously.

"Thanks," I said. "I'm glad I can help."

Our next stop was back toward the center of Revere, at the house Eric and Janice rented on the lower end of Broadway. As we drove along, I opened the envelope with the crime scene photographs and looked carefully at the close-up of the area surrounding Eric's computer monitor. One of them was a tight enough shot to show the University of California seal on his pencil mug. I focused on the little brown cartoon bear that was UC's mascot.

And that's when it jumped out at me.

The arrangement of Eric's figures in the police photograph was not the same as the arrangement on the desk which I'd just seen. I was sure of that.

"Batman is supposed to be in back," I said out loud.

"What's that?" Matt asked.

He turned his eyes from the road and tried to see the photograph. I held it up for him, and pointed to the small black Batman figure.

"The way we just saw Eric's desk," I said, "Batman is hiding the UC bear. And also the rest of these figures are in different places."

We looked at each other for a moment until Matt returned his gaze to the road.

"Someone's rearranged Eric's figures," we said, almost in unison.

Chapter Six

We pulled up in front of the Bensen residence, a large two-story white-shingled duplex set back from the sidewalk. Next to the Bensens' was a run-down apartment building with a makeshift basketball court in the back. Several teenaged boys played in the mild afternoon, their voices loud, their language crude. Within a block of the Bensen house was a fast-food restaurant with drive-up ice-cream service. Although I wouldn't have called it exactly an inner-city slum, I guessed it was not Janice's first choice in neighborhoods.

Matt had called ahead from his car phone to tell Janice we were on our way. I remembered the last time I'd seen her, just before I left California. We'd all gone out to dinner—Leder, Connie, Jim, Eric, Janice, and two other scientists who'd worked on the gas gun. All my suspects, I thought, except for the ones left on the west coast.

I walked in front of Matt up a narrow, sloping driveway, past neat green hedges to the first-floor apartment. Janice greeted us at the door. Although her smile was pleasant, her face twitched like someone in a hurry.

"I have an appointment in an hour," she said, "but I do have some coffee ready." Unlike the Physics Department coffee, this time the aroma was enticing and Matt and I accepted.

We drank our coffee from china cups, sitting on brown leather chairs in Janice's living room. The carpet was a shag, with thick tufts of browns and oranges, echoed in brown and orange wallpaper above stained pine paneling, reminiscent of the earthtone era. The décor didn't fit at all with Janice's usual classy image and I suspected she was still living with the landlord's choices.

In one corner of Janice's living room stood an old maple desk with a pen and sheaves of papers that looked like formal documents spread out, as if its owner had just left a moment ago. I made a mental note to ask Matt if there was any insurance money involved in Eric's death.

I came back to the present and Matt's soothing voice.

"Is there anything in particular you remember about the night Eric was killed?" he asked.

"I don't know what else I can tell you," Janice answered. "I must have been asleep when Eric left the house. He was always slipping out in the middle of the night if he got some idea in his head that couldn't wait."

Her words came out shrill and whiny and I wondered if Janice ever talked in a normal voice. I had to admit this time she had reason to whine, and felt guilty thinking ill of this new widow.

Even in a state of mourning, in her casual black slacks and silk shirt Janice looked ready for a stroll on Boston's Beacon Hill. She had the look of people whose clothes remain perfectly pressed, and never touch their skin even if they do their gardening in them. I scanned her fair complexion for signs of crying and couldn't see any. I did see a fine makeup job and newly coiffed chestnut hair. Probably because Eric was nearly bald, Janice looked a lot younger than her late husband, though I seemed to remember that she'd had her thirtieth birthday.

"It's always awkward to ask this question, Mrs. Bensen," Matt said, "but it's fairly routine in cases like this. I need to know if you thought Eric might be seeing someone else."

"You mean that technician," Janice said, with a shrug of her shoulders, as if Andrea Cabrini were sitting there and needed to be brushed off. "She was infatuated with him, that's all. And Eric probably enjoyed it, as men do."

"So, as far as you know, there was nothing going on between them?"

''Nothing.''

''And in California?''

''What about California?''

Janice wasn't making it easy for Matt, but he remained unflustered, taking time to sip his coffee and dab his mouth with the tiny cloth cocktail napkins Janice had set out.

''Do you think he was seeing someone else in California?''

''No, I don't,'' Janice answered, sounding annoyed. She looked at her watch and then at Matt, but didn't say anything more.

''I think that's all then,'' Matt said. ''In a couple of days you'll be able to collect his things at the lab. I assume you know where to go?''

''Vaguely. I found it very depressing, all those drab walls and clunky equipment, and no light or air from the outside world,'' Janet answered. ''What a place to die.''

Janice put down her cup and walked over to the large bay window facing Broadway. She opened the filmy white curtains as a bus rumbled by and came to a stop at the corner. We were all silent for a moment, as if its noisy brakes had called time-out.

''I could have someone do that job for you,'' Matt said. ''If you'd trust us to take care of everything, we'll bring his things here.''

''Oh, would you? There's nothing valuable really, just his superheroes and his little plastic Einstein.'' A tinny laugh came out of Janice's mouth. I could believe it was a sneer if I hadn't promised myself not to have unkind thoughts.

''We were there today,'' I said. ''He had a beautiful photograph of you on his desk. I'm sure you'll want to keep it.''

''Yes, I saw my picture,'' Janice said. She looked at me and rolled her eyes as if to tell me she got my point. ''I was in his office, if you can call it that, during the department's Memorial Day picnic when we first got back. They had a sort of open house and told us they'd cleaned the lab in our honor—they actually thought it looked ready for visitors. I can't imagine what it must look like in its normal state. I haven't been there since, and if I never go again, it'll be fine."

"We'll take care of it," Matt said. "Please call me if there's anything else we can do or if you think of something that might help us find his killer."

Janice kept her arms folded across her chest and nodded as we said good-bye.

Matt and I left the Bensen house and drove back to Russo's to collect my car. *The moment of reckoning,* I thought, *when he sees my Cadillac.* A real litmus test for relationships.

It was a whole new side of Matt Gennaro that came through as I had him stop at my long black eight-cylinder. He let out the loudest sound I'd ever heard from him—something like whooaaaa—and then confessed.

"I knew what you'd be driving," he said. "Don't forget, my business and Frank Galigani's intersect a lot, and Frank told me about your car deal. I think it's great."

I felt my whole body relax.

"It's a little overwhelming," I said, and then let out a loud laugh of my own.

Matt drove away after asking me to be at the station at ten o'clock the next morning for interviews with Eric Bensen's colleagues, Connie Provenza and Jim Guffy, and Andrea Cabrini if he could reach her.

On my way home in my big car, I tried to replay in my head the sound of Matt's whooping laugh. I also told myself that so far there was not one shred of evidence that Matt thought of me as anything but PSA-6, his sixth Personal Services Agreement this year.

I stopped at the florist across from St. Anthony's and made arrangements for a spray of white chrysanthemums for Eric, the first time I'd ordered funeral flowers to be delivered to my home address. I ordered a separate spray of yellow mums with a card from Elaine and Eric's other friends in California.

* * *

Back at Galigani's, I stopped in at the first parlor. Rose and Frank were there with Martha and the ushers they'd assigned to Eric's wake. The body wouldn't be available for viewing until the weekend, but they were already arranging the room.

''Here's our resident detective,'' Frank said. ''What's new, Gloria?''

With no clients around, Frank dropped his somber voice, but not his impeccable grooming. He almost always wore a dark suit and tie at the mortuary. If our yearbook had a category ''most likely to be an undertaker,'' Frank would have been first choice—always the one to comfort and put things in perspective, calming his friends in the face of teenage traumas.

Since it was close to the end of the workday, I suggested we all go upstairs to my apartment for a snack.

''Great,'' Rose said. ''I made a wine run, just in case you asked.''

While I never remembered to buy wine or beer, I usually had a good supply of fruit and cheese and crackers. Topped off with a good vanilla ice cream, I often considered that dinner.

Martha, whom I knew only slightly, said she had to get home to her children.

''Good luck on the case,'' Martha said before leaving. ''I'm sure you'll crack it.'' Clearly Martha's employers had given her an overblown description of my role in the investigation.

Rose and Frank and I sat around my coffee table with plates of food and got into another memory lane conversation. This time it was about my late fiancé, Al Gravese, and the car crash that killed him just before Christmas in 1962.

''I always thought you'd do more to find out what happened,'' Frank said.

''I might still do that,'' I said.

It was one more thing, like the long walk along the beach, that I'd been putting off. And one more reason my involvement in Eric's murder investigation was such a welcome distraction.

There was talk at the time that Al's death was not an accident. A brief inquiry had turned up nothing suspicious and the matter was put to rest. The gossip was that Al was mixed up with an undesirable element that flourished in the city in the late fifties, local bookies and small-time criminals left over from the bootleg whiskey days.

One of the biggest mysteries of my life was how I'd become engaged to someone I knew so little about. I'd met him while I was a junior in college, several years after Josephine died and I was living alone with my father. Al had come to Revere to work at Rose's father's nursery. He was an expert landscaper and had a passion for the big flower shows in Boston every year.

It was about that time that I'd broken up with Peter, and Al was an attractive, available alternative. He always had a lot of money, and his refusal to tell me what kind of meetings he slipped off to at a moment's notice seemed romantic. I was desired by a rich, mysterious older man—Al was nearly thirty; I was twenty.

Eventually I'd stopped chastising myself for being so naive. It was a different, more private era, I told myself. Not like now, when relationships are the subject of best-sellers and every little intimacy or state of mind gets its own talk show slot.

"If you're interested in doing any research," Frank said, "just tell John. And the young guy who keeps the old files at the newspaper now is a good friend of ours, too. We buried three of his grandparents. He'll give you all the help you need."

"I don't think it's a good idea at all," Rose said, as she did every time the subject of investigating Al's death came up. "If Al really was in some kind of trouble when he died, it could be dangerous to start poking into it. Besides, Gloria's here to start a new life, not to dig up the old one."

As if on cue from the old life, the phone rang. Peter was calling to remind me that I was scheduled to give a talk in his Italian class the next morning. We'd worked out a monthly series of sessions on the contributions of Italians and Italian Americans to science and technology. I'd give a technical presentation in English, and the students would write follow-up papers in Italian on the person's life and times. Not wanting to be tied to chronological order, I'd planned to start with Enrico Fermi and how he achieved the first sustained nuclear chain reaction in 1942.

Once that was settled, Peter invited me to a dinner-dance at Wonderland Ballroom on Saturday night, sponsored by St. Anthony's Knights of Columbus. I told him I wanted to be available to the Bensen murder investigation, and couldn't make plans.

''I'm not happy with this new career of yours,'' Peter said. ''I hope this cop isn't putting you in any danger.''

Something in his tone said ''possessive'' to me, and I responded a little too harshly.

''I'm not doing it to make you happy, Peter,'' I said. ''I'll see you about seven forty-five in the morning. I'll need an overhead projector.''

Rose and Frank were perusing my coffee table museum books, but I could tell that they'd followed the gist of my conversation.

''I think Peter's been waiting for Gloria since 1962,'' Frank said to Rose when I returned to the seating area.

''Well, that's his problem,'' Rose said.

I decided I didn't need to enter into this conversation even if it was about me. We gathered our jackets and purses and I ended up having my second meal of the day at Russo's. There wasn't a lot of choice in our immediate neighborhood, and none of us felt like driving too far.

I asked Frank to drop me off a few blocks before the mortuary so I could take advantage of the perfect weather. I'd been through the toughest part of the year, the hot, muggy summers, and felt that this was a just reward. There was enough of an east wind to carry the smell of salt air inland and I took a deep breath to catch a whiff of the Atlantic Ocean.

I walked at a brisk pace for me, through quiet streets, past rows of one-and two-story houses interspersed with neighborhood markets, repair shops, and cleaners. No California-style strip malls, at least not in this part of Revere. Every time I passed a video store or nail salon, I tried to remember what had been in that spot when I was a child.

I'd already prepared my Fermi talk, but I still had to decide whether to include his flight from Italy with his Jewish wife. Enrico and Laura Fermi went legitimately to Sweden to receive his Nobel Prize, but then directly to America to avoid her persecution. As I walked, I tried to think of a way to relate the experience to a generation that probably hadn't even heard the word "holocaust."

I got home feeling clearheaded and ready for bed. I took a quick look at my e-mail and paper mail and settled on what I'd wear to class, and then to the police station, knowing I wouldn't have time to come home in between.

As I got into bed with a stack of transparencies for one last look at the radioactive decay scheme I'd drawn for my Fermi talk, my phone rang.

A man's voice, but not one I expected.

"This is Ralph Leder," he said. "I want you to know I wasn't pleased with what you were implying this afternoon."

"I'm sorry if I offended you, Ralph, but what exactly is it that bothered you?"

"You know perfectly well what I'm talking about. I'm not going to play games with you. I'm calling to remind you that I have wide-ranging influence in this business. And you're too young to retire completely."

I tried to make a lighthearted response, but it came out tight and high-pitched.

"This sounds like, if-I-ever-want-to-work-in-this-town-again . . ."

"Take it however you want to," he said, and hung up.

Chapter Seven

I've never been a morning person, but after a fitful night it was even harder than usual to get up on Thursday morning. Leder's call shook me more than I thought it deserved. After all, what could he do to me? Poison my name with all the police departments in Boston and vicinity? Call all the schools and cancel my guest appearances?

More important, did this mean he killed Eric Bensen? No, I decided, he couldn't afford to give himself away like that if he were the killer. On the other hand, he couldn't afford not to.

To make the night a complete failure for rest, I kept dreaming of A1. In one vision we were at a flower show in the middle of winter and someone shot him three times right in front of me. In another scene, A1 was being buried under the old high school building.

I forced myself out of bed at six o'clock. I had coffee and a muffin from a batch I'd baked in an attempt to wean myself from stopping at Luberto's Bakery every day.

By seven-thirty, I was parking in the faculty section of the lot behind the high school. The refrain "Cheer Re-vere High" was running through my head, but this building, built long after I'd left, held no nostalgia for me.

It was another clear, sunny fall day, and I watched the students as they lingered outside.

After wrestling with Al's death, Peter's unwanted attention, Matt's apparent disinterest, and Leder's threatening phone call, I found it relaxing to focus on something simple, like nuclear physics.

I met Peter at the main office where I signed in on a clipboard.

I'd chosen a black raw silk suit, black flats, and a hot-pink blouse. From previous experience with high school visits, I knew at least I'd blend in with the many girls who'd be all in black. I wore my standard jewelry for such occasions, a pendant with a hologram, a three-dimensional image of Albert Einstein. My lapel ornament for the day was a tiny bronze likeness of Dante, the pin I'd received as Italian Club secretary in 1958.

Though I knew I'd never be able to stand full-time teaching, I always loved giving talks at schools. An occasional speaker had all the advantages of a guest and none of the disadvantages of maintaining discipline and handling administrative headaches.

"Dr. Gloria Lamerino and I were classmates," I heard Peter say as he introduced me. You'd never guess I'd practically hung up on him twelve hours earlier.

I started my talk with a favorite quote from Enrico Fermi: "Before I came here I was confused about this subject. Having listened to your lecture I am still confused, but on a higher level."

The quote brought the hoped-for laugh and the whole hour went rather well, with thoughtful questions from Peter's students. One asked why scientists did research that might be used for destructive purposes. Another wanted to know about the current status of nuclear power. Several asked me what I thought would be done about the problem of nuclear waste. I did my best to be honest without using the hour as a forum for my political leanings, which were slightly to the left on almost all matters except technology, where I tipped to the right.

By the end of class I was promising to send the students lists of resources for their papers. They knew I'd be back next month to present Galileo Galilei, the sixteenth-century Italian scientist. I teased them with the question of whether Galileo really did investigate gravity by dropping balls of different weights from the leaning tower of Pisa. They'd have to wait a month for the answer.

Peter walked me to my car and leaned on the window ledge as I got settled.

''I'm sorry about last night,'' he said. ''It's just that I worry about you.''

I was proud of myself for not asking him if he'd been worrying for thirty years, or just since I'd been back in his life, for the last two days.

''I'll be fine,'' I said instead, turning my key in the ignition. ''Matt isn't going to let anything happen to me. In fact, I'm going to meet him at ten, so I have to rush.''

Peter straightened up, his shoulders stiffening. ''If you change your mind about the dance, give me a call,'' he said.

''I will.''

Driving off, I asked myself why I'd deliberately made Matt and me sound a lot chummier than we were. The answer had something to do with teenagers and dating, so I dismissed it in a flash.

With just enough time for a cappuccino, I stopped at a new Starbucks at the edge of Revere by the Chelsea border. I used the break to switch my brain from one kind of physical evidence to another. I'd managed to find an old issue of a science magazine that carried the original story of the breakthrough by Leder's group. I looked over the article as I drank my coffee and refreshed my memory of the experimental setup.

Matt was in his office when I arrived, seated behind one of two completely outfitted desks occupying the small space behind a door with a frosted glass window. The other belonged to his partner, George Berger, whom I'd met on previous department visits. My memory of Berger, a short, heavy man in his early thirties, was not pleasant—he'd made it clear from the beginning of my contract that he'd taken physics in high school and chemistry in college and didn't need my help solving a murder.

"You have any experience in detective work?" he'd asked.

"Just a lifetime in scientific research," I'd replied, less confident than my clever remark indicated. It was hard enough for me to get over my feeling of intimidation simply walking into a building full of police officers, in spite of only one moving violation in my thirty-five years of driving. Just as every driver on a California freeway automatically slows down at the sight of a black-and-white highway patrol car, I straightened my shoulders and walked with careful strides every time I entered the tiny high-security vestibule of the Revere police station.

"Here's her résumé," Matt had said that first day, holding out my complete professional history. *Meager,* I thought, fitting on six pages stapled together, hardly more than a page for every ten years of my life. But Matt made a lot of what he had to work with.

"She has everything but the Nobel Prize," he said. "She has all these publications and she's an honorary fellow of three different scientific societies."

Overblown as his summary was, I was grateful to Matt for his support. My preretirement research was of the everyday garden variety, basic experiments on the properties of crystals. Almost every workday for years, I'd plug away at some step in my experimental procedure—zap a small piece of solid crystalline material with a laser, collect the light that bounced off, put the data into a computer, and analyze it for information about the structure of the material. Not even close to brilliant or award-winning, but my perseverance and hard work had paid off with recognition in my narrow specialty of crystal spectroscopy.

Remembering the interaction with Berger, I was happy to find him out of the office as I started work on a new contract. Matt gave me the schedule for the day—Jim Guffy was first, due at ten-thirty, then Connie Provenza after lunch. He hadn't been able to reach Andrea Cabrini, Eric's possible East Coast love interest.

"Let me give you a progress report," he said, his voice soft and comfortable, but sounding more like a bank loan officer than a friend. "First, I got a printout from Casey, our computer guy. I'm not sure it's useful, but I'll get you a copy. Also, since Janice Bensen and Leder have registered guns, we checked them out. Both guns are clean."

I wasn't happy to hear that Leder owned a gun, and it occurred to me that I ought to tell Matt about my bedtime phone call. Not yet, however. Leder didn't threaten me physically, and I didn't want to scare Matt into removing me from the case.

Whenever I could sneak a look, I glanced around Matt's desk and file cabinets for telltale photographs, like a slim young girlfriend framed in a bikini. I knew he hadn't remarried, but not much more about his current status. There was only one picture on his side of the office—an older couple in formal dress seated behind an elaborate cake, presumably his parents at an anniversary celebration.

Matt sat forward in his chair, pulled a yellow pad of paper in front of him, and picked up his pencil.

"One more thing," he said. "The security guard saw a late-model Corvette in the lab parking lot just before midnight. He remembers that it was red and had out-of-state plates, but doesn't remember which state. Sound familiar?"

"No. Not offhand."

"Okay. Let's move to the physics. Can you tell me again exactly what this group has accomplished?" he asked. He'd twisted his nose and set his face into a grimace. Frown lines appeared on his forehead.

"It's not going to be that bad," I said. I thought of reciting the Fermi quote I'd used with Peter's students, but ruled against it. This was serious business that I was getting paid for. I cleared my throat and forged ahead.

"Under normal conditions, like the air temperature and the

pressure in this room, hydrogen is a gas,'' I said, trying to sound friendly, as if I were giving directions to my apartment.

''For at least fifty years scientists have been predicting that hydrogen could be made into a metal if the conditions were right. But they also knew that the so-called right conditions involved extremely high pressures. We've never been able to reach those pressures. But now with lasers and modern electronics, we can create the conditions we need. Are we okay so far?''

''So far.''

''Furthermore, still talking about fifty years ago, they predicted that although it would take extraordinary conditions to produce the metal hydrogen, once it was made, hydrogen would stay a metal even at normal temperatures and pressures.''

Matt had been doodling, but I thought I saw him write an actual word or two during my last sentence.

''And we care about this because . . . ?'' he asked, raising his eyebrows and tapping his eraser on his pad.

''Because if hydrogen can survive as a metal at room temperature, it might be useful as a superconductor—able to conduct electricity with no resistance.''

''And that's where we get these special power lines and the levitated railway trains?'' Matt asked.

''Right,'' I said. ''What Leder's group did was the very first step—they claim to have made metal hydrogen that lasted for about a millionth of a second. No one saw it, of course, but the data in the group's printout says it was there.''

Matt was getting into the swing of things. The frown had left his face, and he sat back.

''So they're saying, 'We made metal hydrogen, so give us money to get to the next step,' '' he offered. ''And the next step after that, way down the road, we'll give you trains that run in the air and perfect utility lines.''

''You've got it.''

''Whoa,'' Matt said, using almost the same nonword as

when he saw my Cadillac. "How do we know they really made it?"

"There's nothing unusual about the way they're making their claim. When we're dealing with something that's so small or lasts for such a short time that we can't see it with our eyes, we have to rely on instruments to detect its existence. This is where Jim's work comes in. He's the experimentalist in the group. Jim's the one who designed the equipment that tells us that metal hydrogen appeared for a brief time."

Matt nodded in a way that gave me hope about his level of understanding, but before we could go any further, Jim Guffy arrived. With his awkward gait, boyish grin, and bright eyes, he had the look of an Irish altar boy. At twenty-something, he wasn't that much older than Peter's students. It was hard to think of him as a potential murderer.

"It's good to see you again," he said to me. He shook Matt's hand and stumbled into the chair next to mine, dropping his sunglasses on my feet.

"Sorry," he said, brushing back thick brown hair. He sat at the edge of the chair, his hands on his knees in a ready-set-go position.

Matt went over Jim's written statement that he hadn't seen Eric since the end of the workday on Monday. He was at an all-day meeting in Boston on Tuesday, he said, and didn't go to the gas gun lab at all. He didn't hear about the murder until lunch break on Tuesday, when everyone was talking about it.

"I just want to make sure I have this right," Matt said. "You live with your parents in Everett?"

"Yes," Jim said, "I was home that night. I mean I was sleeping when Eric, uh . . ."

Jim trailed off, shuffling his feet under his long legs. *If nervousness is a sign of guilt,* I thought, *Jim did it.* Lucky for him, I knew he was naturally shy and uncomfortable in strange situations. And this situation was about as strange as you could get. I also figured that, like me, he was afraid one of the officers in the station would ID him as having made an illegal lane change on Route 1A three years ago.

"Do you remember Eric's saying anything about a discrepancy in the hydrogen data at your party?" I asked.

"No, I don't. I guess I was too busy with the songs."

Jim took his Saint Patrick's Day party seriously. He photocopied the words to dozens of Irish folk songs, with verses no one ever heard before, and we all sang along to the music on CD. It was the only time I'd seen Jim show any signs of leadership.

"But I know a lot of people heard him," Jim said. "Dr. Leder says Eric was drunk."

"Do you know what Eric's supposed problem was?" I asked.

Jim looked down at his brown tassel loafers. "I heard it was about my trigger mechanism," he said. "Eric said the timing of the signal was off."

"You mean 'they say Eric said,' don't you," Matt asked, "since you didn't hear him?"

"Right," Jim said. He looked flustered and nearly dropped his glasses again. "That's what they told me."

After a few more questions, Matt thanked Jim for coming in and encouraged him to call the station if he thought of something that might help the investigation.

Jim let out a deep breath and started out the door. As he passed me, he said, "Neat hologram, Gloria."

"What was that all about?" Matt asked when Jim had left.

"The hologram?"

"That too. But I was thinking about the trigger thing."

"Jim designed a trigger mechanism that produces an electrical signal when the shock wave from the gas gun hits it. A certain measurement at that very moment tells us whether or not the hydrogen has been metallized. It'll be clearer if I draw a diagram."

I reached over to the pad on his desk and noticed several infinities, just like the ones he'd drawn in Leder's office. I wondered if I'd ever know Matt well enough to tease him about that.

"No more science until after lunch," Matt said, leading me

out by my elbow. ''There's a small deli around the corner, unless you have other plans.''

I was starting to worry about the police department food budget, but I didn't let that keep me from agreeing. The deli was almost all counter, with a high refrigerated meat-and-cheese case along the length of it. There was a single row of small round tables along the opposite side, and we got the last one at the back.

The turkey sandwich was good, but no match for Russo's eggplant special. I picked up our conversation, explaining how Eric's computer program would determine when the trigger fired.

''Eric might have seen something in his own program—a line of code that told the trigger to fire at the wrong time. Then the measurement they got would be meaningless.''

''Do we have to do this during lunch?'' Matt asked. ''Tell me about your Einstein picture.''

He looked at my hologram resting on my chest when he said this, sending a pleasant shiver through my upper body. His question also caused me to look again at Albert Einstein and a piece of a puzzle clicked into place. I put down my forkful of oniony potato salad and looked at Matt.

''He's missing,'' I said. ''That's why the figures on Eric's desk were rearranged. Someone took Albert Einstein and covered his tracks by moving the superheroes around.''

''Are you sure?'' Matt asked.

''I'm sure,'' I said. ''Einstein's missing,''

Chapter Eight

As soon as we got back to Matt's office we checked the eight-by-ten color photograph of the area around Eric's computer monitor. The small white figure of Einstein was in front, as I remembered it, to the right of the monitor, next to Batman and the UC mug.

Matt was almost as certain as I was that Einstein was no longer on Eric's desk. He changed our schedule to fit in a return trip to the lab to be sure.

"So much for yellow tape and a police guard," he said. "Whoever did this risked being caught at a crime scene without authorization."

Matt tried reaching Andrea Cabrini again and left a message that he'd look for her in the physics building around four in the afternoon. As I was preparing my notebook for the interview with Connie Provenza, Matt shuffled through pink phone message slips and pulled one out.

"This one's from the security guard at the lab. He's been thinking about the Corvette and is now pretty sure it had Connecticut plates. I'll have to check that out. See if there's anyone from Connecticut in the group, or anyone visiting. Maybe the Physics Department secretary would know."

Matt seemed to be talking to himself, so I waited for a sign to continue our conversation.

"I see that Connie Provenza lives in Chelsea," Matt said. "Before she gets here, can you tell me what her job is in this group?"

He turned over a page on his yellow pad and started to

frown, with his science-is-boring look, but relaxed his face instead. *Maybe I have a convert to physics,* I thought.

"Connie's a theoretical physicist," I told him. "She writes equations, figures out which factors are important in the experiment, and works with Eric on—uh, *worked* with Eric . . ."

I paused and cleared my throat. For the most part I'd managed not to dwell on the fact that someone I knew had been murdered. And the equally distressing fact that most likely someone I knew was a murderer. To be of any help to Matt, I had to think of Eric Bensen's murder objectively, squeezing it into the format of a puzzle, as if it were a question on a science test. Somehow at that moment the reality of death had taken over, keeping me from doing my job.

Matt brought me a cup of water from the cooler outside his office. I hadn't even seen him leave.

"Are you okay?" he asked. "We can do this later."

"I'm fine, thank you, I just needed a minute. You're not getting out of physics class that easily."

Matt laughed and seemed relieved. I wondered if any of his other PSAs broke down in front of him. I wanted to continue, and managed to compose myself.

"Connie worked with Eric on the computer code that represents what's happening to the hydrogen target. She's close to the data, and the most likely one besides Eric to know if something wasn't right with the information coming off the printer."

"Clear enough," Matt said, a little too quickly. "Connie isn't due for another half hour, so why don't we take a break? I have some other things to finish up if you don't mind leaving for a while. Maybe you could take a walk along Broadway?"

I didn't know if this was for my benefit or his, but either way it was a good idea. I left the station, walking past an unpleasant-looking young man handcuffed to a bench in the lobby. A policeman in the dark blue uniform of the RPD was coming toward me, escorting an old man in ragged clothing and a scruffy beard. They entered the same door I was exiting and as we passed I nearly gagged on the odor. *Maybe I'm in the wrong business,* I thought.

But after a refreshing walk along the busy street I got my perspective back. A scoop of mocha almond fudge from the Lantern Dairy helped. As usual, I felt guilty abandoning my resolve to give up desserts until I lost at least ten pounds. I ate right past the feeling, holding the sweet-smelling sugar cone far from my body so I wouldn't spill ice cream on my blouse.

I had a lot of company as I walked, passing men and women in stiff business suits talking about prime rates and real estate. I passed the *Revere Journal* office and interrupted deliveries to several merchants as I stepped around open trap doors in the sidewalk. I didn't recognize anyone and wondered when I would have enough friends in the city to increase the chances of meeting someone I knew on a casual stroll. I was conscious of my walk, my clothing, my accent, anything that gave me away as a "foreigner." At times, in local stores I deliberately tried to drop the final *r* in words like hamburger and sugar, reversing the process I'd gone through when I moved to the West Coast. I felt like I was operating at both ends of a see-saw, constantly missing the equilibrium point in the middle.

The ice cream kept me from going in to any of the shops, but nothing looked that appealing anyway. Most of them offered retail services—dry cleaning, photocopying, TV repair, hairstyling, and the inexplicably popular trend of the nineties, nail sculpture.

I stood in front of a manicure shop done in fake art deco, and watched one young woman paint the fingernails of another. I tried to imagine my mother and her friends having their nails done. Not likely. It was enough of a chore for Josephine to change out of her housedress and slippers now and then for a wedding or graduation. She'd grown up poor and married poor, and was never comfortable with formal dress, by which she meant nylons rolled to her knees and real, closed-in shoes.

Heading back to the police station, I met Connie at the front entrance. When I saw her outfit, a tailored navy-blue suit and pumps, my first thought was that she looked upon this as an important meeting. Like most working scientists, Connie wore jeans and tennis shoes around the lab, in keeping with its construction site décor. The real reason for the business attire, which I estimated to be in size seven, soon became apparent.

"I hope we're finished in time for my management class," she said. "I can't imagine what more I can tell these people. They questioned my boyfriend and Bill wasn't even in town the other night."

"It's really awful about Eric, isn't it?" I said.

It occurred to me after I said it that I was getting very good at sarcasm and reproachful comments. In the last twenty-four hours, I'd made snide remarks to at least four people. I'd suggested to Ralph Leder that he was deceitful, guilty of scientific fraud, and out for money. I'd told Peter Mastrone to lay off after he'd brought me presents and expressed concern over my well-being. I wasn't a bit kind to Janice Bensen whose husband had just been murdered, and now I was being self-righteous with Connie, who was one of my own species, a female physicist. So far only Leder had been rude back to me.

Was I this bad in California? I wondered. I'd have to ask Elaine the next time I talked to her.

Connie didn't take scolding well, and she shot me a look of annoyance, lifting her pointy chin high in the air. I pulled my shoulders back, trying to match her perfect posture. Connie's career-length dark hair and regulation half-inch diameter gold hoop earrings bounced as we walked. I pictured her canceling her subscription to *Science* magazine and writing out checks for business weeklies and money magazines.

"Of course Eric's murder was awful," she said. "That's not my point."

It was just as well that we'd arrived at Matt's office by then, and we took seats in front of his desk.

"Thanks for coming in, Ms. Provenza," Matt said.

"*Dr.* Provenza," Connie said, to my horror. Even in my earliest days, as proud as I was of my doctorate, I wouldn't have corrected anyone that way. Whatever happened to the notion that education was supposed to make us humble? I wondered.

"Excuse me, Dr. Provenza," Matt said with a calmness that I admired. "What I'm most interested in today is anything you can tell me about Eric Bensen and his problem with the data from your group. Dr. Lamerino is here as my interpreter, so to speak."

"Eric was drunk," Connie said. She sat up straight on the chair and, like Jim Guffy that morning, seemed ready to bolt. Unlike Jim, however, Connie didn't seem the least bit nervous. As she elaborated, she kept her chin high and at an angle, her tone not at all like that of a murder suspect, but more like that of a wealthy bank customer who'd come to register a complaint with the manager.

"He was joking," she said. "I can't imagine anyone taking him seriously. If something really were wrong, do you think he'd wait until we're singing 'Danny Boy' to bring it up? Heaven knows we have more than enough meetings for that purpose."

I knew Connie well enough not to be surprised at her tone. I'd never seen her intimidated by anyone, and I saw that homicide detectives were no exception. I chalked it up to her youth. I'd come to the conclusion that my generation of fifty-something women were just now reaching the level of self-confidence and assertiveness that women Connie's age started out with. My liberal intellect told me that was a good thing, but my conservative feelings rebelled. I still hadn't seen what I was looking for—some perfect combination of high self-esteem and a pleasant manner.

"And the last time you saw Eric was when?" Matt asked, seeming less ruffled by Connie's attitude than I was.

"I was with him all day on Monday," she said, "until I left at four for a class. I'm getting my MBA in January."

"I see that," Matt said, running his pencil along a page in the Bensen file. "We just had a report from security at the lab. I'm sure you know Mr. Gallante. He says he saw a late-model red Corvette with Connecticut plates in the lot around midnight.''

For a moment I thought I saw Connie flinch. Not a broad movement, but a definite flinch, a slight twitching of her shoulders and a brief flush to her face. *If this is what it seems,* I noted, *Connie needs more practice before negotiating in the boardroom with the good old boys.*

Matt must have noticed it, too. He leaned forward.

''Do you know that car, Dr. Provenza?'' he asked. It may have been wishful thinking, but I thought I detected a slight emphasis on the word ''Doctor'' that time.

''No,'' Connie said, ''I drive a red 'seventy-three BMW.''

Matt nodded, then read a few more sections of Connie's statement to her and asked three or four general questions.

''Can you think of anyone who'd want to kill Eric?''

''No, of course not. I mean, I've never known anyone who was murdered or did a murder.''

''Have you ever seen him arguing with anyone?''

''Dr. Leder, which we've already discussed. And he bickered with his wife. But don't we all? Bicker, I mean.''

Connie had mellowed considerably since the red Corvette question. She'd adopted a cooperative spirit and took her time answering Matt's new questions, even calling him Sgt. Gennaro at one point.

''Do you think Eric and Andrea Cabrini were having an affair?'' Matt asked.

''Poor Andrea adored Eric, but I can't see them sl . . . I don't think it was an affair.''

''What about on the West Coast?'' Matt asked. ''Do you think he was seeing anyone while he was out there?''

Connie sat back and ran her tongue around her teeth, staring at her polished navy pumps as if deep in thought.

''I don't know,'' she said. ''Eric was a flirt, I suppose, although never with me. Not like Dr. Leder, if you know what I mean. Eric was just friendly.''

''Anyone he was particularly friendly with?''

''No, not really.''

I made a note to call Elaine and ask her if she thought Eric had a girlfriend in California, although I couldn't imagine she wouldn't already have told me something like that. Elaine had edited one of Eric's short technical memos and saw him often for several weeks. She'd also come on one or two of our dinner excursions.

''I think that's all, Dr. Provenza. Thanks for coming in,'' Matt said.

Once again comparing Connie to Jim Guffy, I determined that Connie's sigh of relief as she left to go was at least as loud as Jim's.

''Interesting,'' Matt said, when she was gone. ''The Corvette got a rise.''

Matt seemed to be talking to himself again, at the same time writing on a sheet of paper in Connie's file. I had the feeling he thought I'd left with Connie—*Dr. Provenza,* I reminded myself with an internal tsk-tsk.

''Maybe she responded that way because she has a red car,'' I said, to alert him to my presence so he wouldn't inadvertently reveal any private thoughts. ''Maybe at first she thought you meant her red BMW.''

''Could be,'' he said. He looked up at me and scanned my face, as if he were holding a Geiger counter or on the lookout for radiation damage. ''Are you ready for more, or would you like to call it a day? We can put off the lab visit for another day, Dr. Lamerino.''

That time there was a definite emphasis on ''Doctor'' and I responded in kind.

''I'm just getting started, *Sergeant* Gennaro,'' I said, with the brightest smile I could manage. *Our first shared joke,* I thought with a shiver of contentment. It flashed through my mind that the idea of visiting a murder scene with Matt brought more smiles to my face and warmth to my heart than the thought of dinner-dancing with Peter.

Chapter Nine

Matt drove north along Broadway to Squire Road, the main westbound thoroughfare. As we headed toward Charger Street to the lab, we kept the conversation on the case at hand except for a few remarks about the changing weather. The sky had darkened considerably and we guessed it was the end of our long string of two sunny days. Matt had thrown an umbrella and a wrinkled beige raincoat like Columbo's in the back of his car before we left.

"It must be the wake and funeral," Matt said. "Doesn't it always rain at cemeteries?"

"It certainly seems that way. Do you plan to attend the services for Eric," I asked, "or does that only happen on TV?"

The idea of Matt below, if not in, my apartment at Galigani's had been fluttering around my brain for a while. I wondered about the protocol of asking him up for coffee afterward. *No middle ground,* I thought. *Either I'm broken up about Eric's death and can't even talk, or I'm plotting to use his wake as a fast track to a romantic rendezvous.*

"One of us will go. I was thinking of getting my partner over there. You remember George Berger?" Matt said. "His wife had a baby this week."

I wasn't sure whether Matt really forgot about my interaction with Berger, or he was testing my ability to get along with others, as measured by reports from day-care providers.

"How nice. Their first child?" I asked, showing magnanimous goodwill and forgiveness.

"The first one, and they're both wrecks. George says it's worse than a stakeout for irregular sleeping patterns."

"Does he know anything about this case yet?" I asked.

"No, that's why I might see if I can get him started. Unless we solve this case by Monday. What are you doing this weekend?"

I nearly jumped in feet first, making a fool of myself by suggesting dinner and a movie. Narrow escape, but I realized in time that Matt was talking about working, not socializing.

"I'll clear my calendar," I said.

We both laughed and I guessed that it dawned on Matt after he said it that his question could be taken two ways. He kept his eyes on the road, looking straight ahead.

"What ever made you go into physics?" he asked.

Just like a man, I thought, casting a vote for sexism. *Ask the first almost-personal question while you're driving and you don't have to make eye contact.* It had started to rain and the windshield wipers provided an extra level of noise to eliminate any possibility of intimacy. I decided to keep my response equally objective and factual.

"I had two excellent women science teachers in high school," I said. "A definite statistical rarity for those days, but I didn't know any better. I thought all scientists were women, and they encouraged me. So I just kept studying math and physics."

"Are you glad to be back in Revere?"

I almost said, "This must be what it feels like to be one of your suspects," but although he had one of the friendliest faces I could imagine, I still wasn't comfortable joking with Matt.

"I'm still thinking about that," I said. "I came back almost on an impulse, just the way I left a long time ago."

"I know," Matt said. "Frank told me a little about the circumstances, how you were engaged to Al Gravese. Not that I was prying. It's just that it's pretty unusual for someone to leave a town and return thirty-one years later."

"I don't have any dramatic reasons or big secrets," I said, "just some strange decisions in my life, I guess."

I neglected to mention that I was happy he'd thought of me as a real human being with a history he was interested in. I'd been working on the assumption that I didn't exist for Matt before I met him in June.

"I remember the crash and the investigation. I'd just joined the force," he said.

I almost asked whatever made him join the force, but I was afraid he'd think me sarcastic. *I* thought me sarcastic, so it wasn't a great leap to guess that others did. I continued to play it straight.

"A couple of nights ago I was looking through some clippings that I'd kept at Galigani's all these years," I said. "It's possible that I came back to find some resolution, to satisfy myself about how he died."

"You mean you think the crash wasn't an accident?"

"Not necessarily, but whatever it was, I ran away from it, and now I need to face it."

With that explanation, as muddy as the lab parking lot on this rainy Thursday, our time in the car was up. In one way, I was sorry we'd arrived since I wanted to bare my soul to Matt and see his in return. In another way, I was grateful for the interruption. As we shared Matt's enormous black umbrella on our walk to the lab entrance, we switched to talk of Eric's murder investigation.

"Let's go downstairs first," Matt said, "and check out the toys on the desk." He held the envelope with the crime scene photographs close to his chest, under the umbrella.

We entered through the basement, dark and shadowy even in the middle of the day, and went down the ramp to the gas gun lab. Since Eric's desk was so close to the edge of the ramp, as soon as we opened the door we could see that the lineup of figures didn't match the photographs. And Einstein was missing.

"Okay," Matt said, as if he were checking off items on a

mental list. "I guess your scientific eye is good for a lot of things."

"I'm sure you would have seen it," I said, trying to hide my pleasure. If nothing else, maybe I was earning my money.

We left the lab and went up to the second floor.

A very heavy woman in jeans was sitting on a long wooden bench in the corridor outside the department office, a white lab coat stretched across her wide hips. The woman was looking down at a clipboard on her lap, snapping the metal clip up and down. Her hair, in many shades of brown, fell in curly disarray around her shoulders.

She looked up as we approached and I was surprised to see a fresh young face above the matronly body. She stood up and clutched the clipboard to her generous bosom.

"Are you the police?" she asked.

"Detective Gennaro," Matt said, casually showing his badge. "Andrea Cabrini?"

"I'm Andrea Cabrini," she said, her voice heavy with resignation. At that moment she seemed ready to raise her wrists for handcuffing.

Here's someone too large even for my *wardrobe,* I thought, *and probably only about twenty-five years old.* So much for Leder's comment about "our little technician." And so much for stereotyping what "the other woman" would look like. I wondered if Andrea's size was also the reason Connie couldn't picture Eric sleeping with her. I considered Connie a good candidate for the pool of people who think only the young and fit can have fun.

Matt introduced me and told Andrea he'd like to ask her a few questions.

"Is there somewhere we can talk?" he asked.

"I have a cubicle downstairs but it's roped off. I've been using the library."

"Why don't we go down to your cubicle?" Matt said. "It's time to remove the tape anyway."

"Dr. Leder will be glad to hear that," Andrea said.

"I'll bet you're glad, too," I said.

She let out a sigh. "I guess so."

This time we took the elevator and approached the ramp door from a different direction. On the way, Matt asked Andrea what her work was in the lab.

"I'm just the technician for the group," she said "After I got my bachelor's degree, I needed money so I took this job. I might go back to school later. Right now I build chassis, do all the wiring, and maintain the equipment. I work with Jim Guffy mostly."

Once inside the large lab room, Andrea led us to her cubicle, two past Eric's. She walked by Eric's desk without looking at it and dragged chairs from the center of the room into her space. An assortment of sweaters and jackets on a coat rack in one corner partly covered a periodic table of the elements tacked to the wall. Andrea's desk looked more like a workbench, strewn with tiny electronic components, wire cutters, circuit diagrams, and rolls of multicolored cable.

Once seated, Matt took out his traveling pad, a small spiral-bound notebook like the kind stenographers use. Andrea stood her clipboard upright on her sloping lap and leaned on it. In spite of her size, she looked like a child about to take a spelling test she hadn't prepared for.

"When was the last time you saw Eric Bensen?" Matt asked.

"Monday," Andrea said. "I said good-bye to him about five o'clock when I left."

"How close were you and Eric?" Matt asked.

His voice had a nonchalant ring, hardly in keeping with the significance of the question, and the answer. I waited.

"I'm sure everyone's told you or you wouldn't be here," Andrea said. "When the first policeman didn't ask me, I thought I was safe." Andrea's voice was high-pitched, coming from a tiny mouth buried in the mounds of flesh that were her cheeks.

"Safe from what?" Matt asked.

"Talk, suspicion," she said. "Eric and I were good friends. We weren't lovers, if that's what they told you."

"Why do you think anyone would say you were lovers?" Matt asked.

I was feeling out of place with this line of questioning, but decided Matt knew what he was doing and would have told me if he wanted to be alone with Andrea.

"Because we hung out together, I guess, and we gave each other little cards and presents. I knew he was just flirting with me, because Janice is so unloving." She stopped for a minute and caught her breath. "I shouldn't have said that. Janice is a good person. She's just always picking at Eric, even in front of his friends."

"Do you have a lot of contact with Mrs. Bensen?"

"Not that much, she came to the Memorial Day picnic and open house, and sometimes we all have breakfast together in the cafeteria on days when she drops him off."

"Did you ever see Eric alone outside the lab?"

"No," Andrea said, dragging out the vowel sound as if she'd been accused of stealing candy from the corner drugstore. "It wasn't like that. I knew once he got his degree he'd move away and I wouldn't see him again. I think he had a girlfriend in California, too. I used to hear him whispering into the phone. My roommate says he was using me, but I just enjoyed him while I had him."

Matt looked away as Andrea started to cry.

"Eric was really nice to me," she said, drying her eyes with a tissue she'd dug out of her pocket. "He was my friend."

In an effort to be as unintrusive as possible, I looked beyond Andrea, my eyes on the wall above her head where a large sepia poster of Einstein riding his bicycle was held up by pushpins. Before I could weigh the merits of asking the question, I had already blurted it out.

"Did you give him the little figure of Einstein?" I asked.

She looked at me as if I'd just looked into a crystal ball and come up with her life. Matt kept his eyes on his notepad.

"Yes," she said, making no attempt to hide her amazement.

"Did you also take it back?" Matt asked, not missing a beat.

Andrea's eyes widened and her clipboard fell from her lap. *She probably figures we were both sent by the devil,* I thought.

"Yes, I took it back," she said. "I know I wasn't supposed to come in here, but it was the last thing I gave him. For his birthday. And I wanted it as a remembrance. I messed up the other figures so no one would notice, but I guess it didn't work."

Andrea was still sniffling and blew her nose at the end of each sentence, her tissue ending up in shreds.

"How did you get in here?" Matt asked, as if he were merely curious and not taking notes for his murder book.

"One of my roommates got the guard to leave for a couple of minutes. She told him there was a problem in the parking lot. I don't want her to get into trouble. It was my fault."

She's not the only one in trouble, I guessed, thinking of what might happen to a police guard who leaves his post. Remembering all the create-a-diversion plots I'd seen in movies, I pictured Andrea's roommate in a short leather skirt and fishnet stockings tottering on red sandals with four-inch heels.

"Just one more question, Ms. Cabrini," Matt said, "and we'll let you get back to work. Do you know why anyone would want to kill Eric?"

"No, I just know *I* didn't. I loved him." she said, her voice barely a squeak. Andrea looked at me, her eyes narrow slits above the padding of her cheeks. "I didn't kill him," she said.

For what it was worth, I patted her soft wide shoulder as we left.

When we reached the top of the ramp, Matt approached the policewoman and I heard him ask for a list of the men who shared the crime scene duty. I walked ahead to give them privacy as he continued to talk to her and write in his notebook.

After a few minutes, I saw her gather up the yellow tape as Matt caught up with me and we walked in silence back to his car.

Chapter Ten

After a day that began with too little sleep and ended with an emotional interview, I was glad to be home. By six o'clock I'd changed into jeans and my Fisherman's Wharf sweatshirt and was settled in my glide rocker with 1950s instrumental music and a cup of coffee. My thinking scenario.

As "Autumn Leaves" rippled through my living room, my first thought was that Andrea had demonstrated more grief than Janice had—by an order of magnitude. But I knew that outward signs didn't necessarily have anything to do with a person's true feelings. I thought back to my response to Al's death. I'd been too shocked to cry, which kept me from falling apart publicly. I went around for a while looking and feeling like the universe had contracted to a small, cold core. It wasn't until many months later when I was in California that I felt the release of several long outbursts of sobbing.

"You need to join a support group," Elaine Cody had told me, in the fashion of Berkeley in the sixties. "I'm sure there's one for young widows. Which you are, sort of."

I'd met Elaine, who was already working as a technical editor, soon after I arrived in California for graduate school. I got over my trauma in a reasonable amount of time thanks to her good humor, mind-wrenching physics homework assignments, and the threat of having to sit on the floor in a circle and share my inner life with strangers.

Thirty years later, I still wasn't much better at sharing my inner life, I realized, shutting up like an unwilling Revere

Beach clam whenever anyone tried to help me work things out, even Rose.

I forced myself out of my rocker and had a meal of pasta and vegetables created out of supplies I'd picked up at a market perilously close to Luberto's Bakery. Even after eating I was in a low-energy state and at loose ends.

I looked at my desk where I'd put the printout from Eric Bensen's computer and considered working on it. I was also tempted to review my notes and reevaluate all the main suspects, but I knew I needed a break from the murder investigation. I thought of taking a walk until I heard the cold rain beat against the windows of my apartment. While I fantasized about rainy walks on the beach, when it came right down to it I preferred dry ones.

I decided to call Elaine and find out if she'd been aware of a girlfriend in Eric's California life. I reached her at work, at just after three in the afternoon on the West Coast.

''Is everything okay?'' she asked.

I knew this deviation from our routine Saturday-or Sunday-morning call, combined with Eric's murder, was throwing Elaine off kilter.

''Just a quick question,'' I said. ''Did you ever hear of Eric having an affair out there?''

''Gloria, you never pay attention. Remember Annie Lee, the young Korean woman who could barely speak English?''

''The one who worked in the department office?''

''Right. Eric hung around her a lot and people talked. But I'm pretty sure it wasn't really an affair. Annie had hardly any friends and I think she just enjoyed the attention.''

''How could you tell?''

''Gloria, when you're in the library and you see a guy sitting next to a woman and he's playing with the sleeves of her sweater, you don't have to be a genius . . .''

''Okay, I get it. I guess I was never in the library when they were both there.''

''Right,'' Elaine said, with a humorous twist to her voice.

Elaine had made her point. I always missed subtle interactions in my social circle. Eric certainly wasn't the typical Lothario in looks, with a small frame, thinning hair, and bifocals, but it was beginning to sound as if he had carved out his niche—find a young woman isolated from society for one reason or another, and give her some harmless thrills. And feed your own ego, I threw in, to complete my unsolicited psychological profile of the murder victim.

"Thanks, Elaine," I said. "Sorry to bother you at work."

"No charge," she said with a laugh, and we hung up.

For the next few minutes I gave in to nostalgia for my life in California, with Elaine, a familiar daily routine, and no murders. No matter which coast I was on I seemed to prefer the other. I wondered when I'd stop blaming Josephine for giving me no practice making decisions or figuring out my own likes and dislikes.

I came back to the present and thought about whether I should tell Matt about Annie Lee. Girlfriends didn't fall within the scope of technical aspects of the investigation, and I didn't want him to think I was overstepping the limits of my contract. On the other hand, I wanted him to think I was on top of things. I resorted to my usual decision-making strategy—postponement.

Energized by my little talk with Elaine, I thought I could manage a sorting and tossing mission to the attic. It was time to make some decisions about what I'd left up there. Putting my box cutter in my pocket, I walked through a door in my bedroom, into the narrow hallway at the back of my apartment. A strange architectural feature of the building, the hallway ran most of the length of my bedroom and living room. Looking at the layout, I got the impression that the carpenters had made a two-foot mistake in following the building plans and decided to make the difference into a foyer for the attic.

I dragged a short ladder down the corridor to a point under the trapdoor. The top of the ladder, specially designed for entry to the attic, had small hooked ends that fit into grooves on the attic floor on one side of the opening. I jiggled the ladder until the hooks clicked into place and climbed up.

Although the Galigani family had never lived in the mortuary building, its attic had become the musty storage place for torn-up luggage, cast-off baseball bats, and rubber swords from old Halloween costumes. And dozens of cartons in storage for old friends on the road.

I pulled the chain next to the bare bulb hanging from the ceiling. Not much improvement in illumination, but I ignored the strong temptation to leave the attic and return to it in the daylight. As I walked back through cobwebs and dust toward my boxes, crouching under the low ceiling, I heard the phone ring in my bedroom below me. By the time it reached my ears, the ringing mingled with the sounds of boards creaking and rain hitting the attic window and roof, the eerie symphony leaving me with a sense of isolation. It seemed a great distance to the real world of good illumination and technological contact with other people.

I knew I didn't have time to reach the phone even if I hurried down, so I let the answering machine take over and made a resolution to carry the cordless phone with me on my next trip to the upper regions of the house. Once that was settled in my mind, I turned to my task.

My boxes were identical brown cartons, marked with long-forgotten codes. I could only guess that the box labeled PT60-4 contained four years of back issues of one of my favorite magazines, *Physics Today*. I knew that the two with AG in wide black letters were about Al Gravese. He'd been living with his parents in the North End of Boston when he died, so the only things I had were souvenirs and presents from him or items that he might have left around my home.

By the time I met Al, Josephine had died and I was sharing a bottom-floor apartment in a duplex with my father on Tuckerman Street, a hilly road not far from the current Bensen residence. Often after a late night with me or business of his own, Al bunked upstairs with the Corrados, the old couple who owned the house.

I could almost hear Mrs. Corrado's broken English. "You

got a nice boy,'' she'd tell me, with as much of a twinkle as her watery old eyes could hold.

In the four months since I'd been back in Revere, I'd gone through only three or four boxes, all with codes other than AG. I'd found my high school yearbook, the dust of years embedded deep in the crevices of the embossed replica of Paul Revere's lantern that was its logo. For some inexplicable reason, I'd also kept a collection of essays in Italian that had won me a prize in the Sons of Italy contest, and a crinoline petticoat, most of which had disintegrated into a pile of dry white flakes.

It was time to dig deeper, I decided. I dragged the box marked AD#1 under the light bulb and slit open the top. My fingers sifted through enough dried flowers to line a casket and picked out a sour-smelling brown photograph album. I took a seat on a rickety director's chair by the small attic window and put the dusty book on my lap.

All the pictures I had of Al were in the album. I'd left it behind in Revere and hadn't seen it since. I took a deep breath, and flipped through the black pages, made of thick construction paper. I looked at dozens of photographs in front of the same background. First me on the sand at the beach, then Al in the same spot, then a whole group. I paused over a few pictures with Rose and Frank at a flower show and other couples whose names I couldn't remember. *Enough of this,* I thought. *I'll try another box.*

I repacked the first carton and slit open AG#2. Everything in this box was contained in a wrinkled brown paper bag sealed with transparent tape, yellow and cracked with age. Along the side of the bag was written, *from M. Corrado,* in the oddly curled script of people from the old country. I barely remembered getting this bag from our landlord right after Al's funeral. It seemed I'd stuffed it in a box without even opening it. From the weight and feel of it, I guessed it held clothing.

I opened the bag and pulled out three shirts that I recognized as Al's. There was a toothbrush, a dark green chenille robe, some socks and underwear, and a square-faced travel clock in a plain silver case. The clothing had a putrid smell that did nothing for the already dank air of the attic. *This one's easy,* I thought. *Give the clock to the Salvation Army and toss everything else.*

As I shook out the robe a small object fell onto my lap—a tiny address book, not more than three inches long and two inches wide, with a black leather cover, brittle and dry. The pages were in good shape for their age and as I leafed through them, I saw line after line of names and numbers in Al's handwriting. Some of the numbers were obviously phone numbers, others had dollar signs next to them.

I sat back on the floor and tapped the book against my leg. I groaned out loud, tapped a few more times, and put the book in my pocket for a later decision.

By ten o'clock my knees were hurting and I decided to go downstairs and soak in my tub. In the old days at ten o'clock Al and I and Rose and Frank might be just starting an evening together, heading out for an all-night diner. But my knees didn't hurt then, either.

I carried a glass of water and the latest *New Yorker* magazine into my bedroom, counting on the cartoons for complete distraction from decisions about my belongings and from the emotional lows of the day.

As I placed my glass on the nightstand, I noticed the blinking light on the answering machine. For all the nervousness it produced at the time, I'd forgotten about the call that came in while I was in the attic. I pushed the button on top of the unit and heard Rose's voice.

"Hi, hope you had a good day," she said, her voice too cheerful for the message to come. "I just want to tell you not to worry if you hear noise downstairs tonight. The guys will be moving Eric Bensen's body into the first parlor around midnight. Have a good night. Talk to you later."

Chapter Eleven

I'd become accustomed to living two floors above dark parlors where corpses appeared regularly. Galigani's was one of only three funeral homes in a city of nearly forty-five thousand people, so they had "clients" as they called them at least four days out of every seven. On my first night in the apartment I had to walk past a small white casket holding the body of a stillborn baby girl. Images of the grieving young parents and the tiniest pale pink flowers I'd ever seen haunted me for days.

But this was my first experience living in the same building as the wake of a friend, a murdered one at that. Another restless night, with dreams of cardboard coffins falling apart in rainy graveyards. The shifty-eyed rats I hadn't met in the attic visited my subconscious in the middle of the night. I stayed in bed until almost ten o'clock on Friday morning, lazily sipping coffee, to make up for a busy, nerve-racking dream life.

Since I wasn't due at Matt's office until one-thirty, I used the rest of the morning to catch up on some other work. I had to finish a junior high science education project on lasers for a San Francisco science museum, and in three weeks I was scheduled to speak at a high school physics club meeting.

I'd deliberately arranged my physics club talk for November seventh, the common birthday of two of my heroines, Marie Curie in 1867 and Lise Meitner in 1878. I planned to open with the story of the first meeting between Meitner and the other great nuclear physicist, Ernest Rutherford.

"Oh," he'd said as a greeting, "I thought you were a man."

Having been nearly invisible at many physics conferences myself, I had no trouble believing the anecdote—that Rutherford was unaware of Meitner's gender although he had read her publications and followed her research with interest.

I sat down with my third cup of coffee and started my yearly reading of my favorite biography of Marie Curie, written by her younger daughter, Eve. I thought again what a wonderful, simple realm of reality physics provided. Eric's murderer couldn't possibly be another physicist, I told myself again, and revisited the temptation to rule out Leder, Connie, and Jim for that reason alone.

Just before eleven o'clock Rose called up to me on the intercom that connected the three floors at Galigani's Mortuary.

"How are you doing?" she asked. "Have you seen Eric?"

For the second question, Rose went into her graveside voice. After years in the business, she moved easily from her normal light tones to her compassionate business voice. Anyone listening to her would know that Eric was lying dead in a funeral parlor, and not someone you might have seen walking along Broadway that morning.

"No, I'd rather not go in until the family sees him," I said.

"Frank did a good job," Rose said.

"I'm sure he did," I said. I remembered Frank's pride when he first worked out a formula that gave the skin of his corpses a more lifelike color. He added a pink dye to the formaldehyde mixture and was able to eliminate much of the heavy makeup I saw at most viewings. Every time I paid my respects to shapeless faces with crusty orange makeup I renewed my resolution to be cremated. I hadn't told that to Rose and Frank yet.

"Peter called to see if Frank and I wanted to join you two at the Wonderland dance tomorrow night," Rose said.

I clenched my teeth and rubbed at a dull ache that had taken over my face around my jaw, scowling at the now-droopy roses Peter had brought as if they'd betrayed me. I decided not to continue the conversation with Rose in the bent-over position I'd assumed in order to use the intercom, which was at the back of my desk.

"Why don't you come on up?" I said. "I'll give you lunch and the short form of my feelings in that regard."

"Will do."

I gave Rose the recent history of my interactions with Peter, feeling as though we'd reverted to our days of whispering about boys in the girls' room.

"I always knew Peter had more than one reason for maintaining a friendship with me and Frank all these years," Rose said. "Not that we didn't get along, but I knew he was using us to keep up with what you were doing."

I let out a long sigh, as if we were fifteen and Rose had just told me that the kid with the most pimples in homeroom liked me and wanted to take me to the senior prom. *If we're going to do this,* I thought, *we might as well go all the way.*

"What do you know about Matt Gennaro?" I asked.

"Aha," Rose said. "Now we're getting somewhere."

"What do you mean by that?"

"Come on, Gloria, it's time you grew up a little in that area."

"I don't think I like the way this is going."

"You don't have to. Just let me take care of it."

I knew Rose was right. I did need to figure out what if anything I was going to do about my love life. While I lived in California, I'd had what might be called dates, mostly arranged by Elaine, but not many, and never past the stage of a good-night kiss. I'd been Elaine's maid of honor twice and saw her through two divorces. *Not much inspiration for trying myself,* I'd mused, conveniently ignoring the successful decades-long Galigani marriage.

By now I was flushed and pacing up and down on the four-foot paisley runner between my entryway and living room. I faced Rose's direct attack head on.

"Let's have lunch," I said.

I wandered into the kitchen, Rose at my heels, and pulled

out the makings of sandwiches and a mini salad bar. Rose kept at it while she made the coffee.

''I'm not talking about a big deal,'' Rose said. ''Frank knows Matt. We buried his wife ten years ago. Genetic heart disease. That's why they didn't have children. Very sad.'' Rose paused to acknowledge the tragedy of a woman dying in her forties. It was the first I'd heard about how and when Matt's wife had died. I wanted to know more but refrained from asking follow-up questions. Rose was in enough of a hurry to get us together. ''Frank would know if he's seeing anyone at the moment,'' Rose continued. ''If not, we can invite him for a simple dinner at our house.''

''And I just happen to be there?'' I pulled at a head of lettuce, tearing it apart with my bare hands. I imagined a simple meal at Rose's, with her Spode china, fine crystal, and monogrammed silverware resting on her grandmother's lace tablecloths. Although they never commented on my supermarket stemware, bought in packages of six in cardboard cartons with handles, Rose and Frank didn't have it in them to entertain casually.

''We'll tell him ahead of time. People do this all the time, Gloria.''

Rose emphasized the word ''people.'' It was clear that she meant the large group of normal, romantically active adults, of which I was not a member.

''It'll be so obvious,'' I said, surprised that I didn't just say no.

''Well, what if it is? We're all adults. He can refuse and nothing's lost.''

''Except my face and my dignity. No, I don't think so.''

I pictured myself in Matt's office the day after he told Frank he wasn't interested in a ''double date.'' I didn't like the picture.

''I'm sorry I mentioned him,'' I said. ''We're working together. That's all.''

''Right.''

Rose sighed and picked up a paring knife with her right

hand and a cucumber with her left. She waved the cucumber in my direction.

"I know this isn't just about Al's memory," she said. "You're smarter than that."

"I'm too old," I said, in a voice so weak I was amazed that Rose heard me. The beige tiles of my kitchen counter seemed to turn to a liquid, like very weak tea, blurring my vision so that I lost focus, and Rose's voice seemed to come from far away.

"I'm going to forget you said that. I'm also going to wait until this case is over, since you have to work with Matt. Then we'll get serious."

I recovered my poise, such as it is, and watched as Rose scored the skin of the cucumber, then put it on the cutting board and sliced it at an angle until she had a neat row of identical oval pieces with ridged edges. She didn't speak for several minutes, her jaw set, her small oval face a study in concentration. I'd seen it before. She'd gone into her long-range planning mode.

We called down to Frank and invited him up for lunch.

"Not a word," I said to Rose.

She put her index finger on her bright-red lower lip and shook her head. As a promise that gave me confidence, the gesture fell short.

Frank came into the room and gave us each a kiss. "Smells good," he said. "And I think you'll be happy with how your friend looks, Gloria." I wondered how long it had taken him to be able to speak of food and corpses in same breath.

Frank removed his dark-brown suit jacket and hung it in the hall closet with great care. "The Bensens just arrived to view Eric and they seem satisfied."

"Are they still down there?" I asked, relieved to have the conversation on a new track, away from my social life.

"Yes," Frank said, "Eric's parents and his wife are having some private time now. Then we'll talk about tonight's program."

Frank's voice was like a soft hymn by a church organist.

He rolled up his starched white shirtsleeves as if he were folding an altar cloth at St. Anthony's, and filled his plate from the small buffet Rose and I had laid out on my counter.

From the amount of food I'd seen Frank consume at various meals together, it wasn't clear to me how he kept his short frame looking firm and trim. As far as I knew the only physical activity he engaged in was golf, and I always thought of that as more of a networking activity than a bodybuilding sport. Unlike Frank, I could see every calorie I consumed, easily identifiable on my body. In fact, my baby fat was still intact.

"So, tomorrow night, are you ready to dance your shoes off?" he asked me.

Rose looked at me and showed me her palms in an attitude of helplessness.

"We've had a change of plans," she said to Frank. "I'll tell you later."

Frank didn't pursue the topic, and I envied the way long-term partners in life and in work communicated without lengthy explanations.

Rose and Frank left to go back to work at twelve-thirty, leaving me only an hour to dress and get to Matt's office. The rain had stopped during the night, but it was colder than it had been all week. I discarded the idea of a short-sleeved silk dress and put on a three-piece gray-and-white-striped knit outfit that I thought would also do for the wake in the evening. I rummaged around my pin collection and selected a pewter cable car about an inch long, that fit along the edge of the jacket. *If I were in San Francisco now,* I thought, *I'd wear my silver Old Ironsides pin.*

I left my apartment and walked down the front stairs toward the parlor where Eric was laid out. I wasn't looking forward to seeing him dead, no matter how good he appeared to my funeral director friends.

Since there was no one with Eric's body except two men from Galigani's staff, I walked in across the dark carpet. The air in the room was saturated with the smell of gladioli, lilies, and chrysanthemums, in wreaths and baskets arranged around the casket. Three tall vases of red roses in front were wrapped in long white ribbons with gold foil letters attached. *Beloved Husband. Loving Son. Grandson.* On either side of Eric's casket were other baskets of flowers, among them my own bouquet and the second one I'd ordered, from his California friends.

I approached Eric's body, kneeled on the wooden prie-dieu, and leaned my arms on its gold velvet top. A metal rack with new cream-colored votive candles stood next to the prie-dieu. Heavy burgundy curtains had been drawn across the windows, and the room was as dark as it would be in the middle of the night.

It was strange to see Eric in a suit and tie, lying still, without his thick glasses. The lining of his cherrywood casket was stark white, the only source of brightness in the room. I looked at Eric's slightly protruding upper lip, so true to life, and remembered the mini-lecture Frank had given me on how photographs of clients when they were alive helped the embalmer reconstruct their faces in death. Frank seldom had a chance to talk about his work outside the family and was hard to stop when he thought someone was interested, which for some strange reason, I was.

I was surprised to see a black crystal rosary wrapped around Eric's fingers. I didn't remember that Eric or Janice ever went to church and I wondered whose idea it was to put prayer beads in his hands.

I drew in a deep breath and allowed my mind to wander. I thought about Eric's life in the gas gun lab, the data he'd added to our information about the elements of the universe, the people he loved. I hoped that either there was some afterlife he might enjoy, or there wasn't and it didn't matter. I considered how different my prayer life had become since my youth as a communicant in St. Anthony's parish. *Maybe my prayer for Eric is taking the form of helping find his murderer,* I thought, with a sudden hopeful feeling.

When I heard voices on the landing by Frank's office on the second floor, I moved quickly out of the parlor, like an intruder caught in the act.

I left the building and went around the side to the garage. As I pulled out onto the street in my Cadillac, I saw Janice Bensen and an older couple, whom I took to be Eric's parents, leave the mortuary. I paused in the driveway, hoping they wouldn't look back and see me, preferring to meet them when they were ready for guests, later that evening.

The older couple were talking to each other while Janice walked in silence several yards behind. The couple drove off in a late-model maroon Oldsmobile. Janice got into an old blue Toyota parked across the street and drove away in the opposite direction.

As far as I could tell, there were no good-byes.

Chapter Twelve

Walking down the hall toward Matt's office I realized I still hadn't looked at the computer printout he'd given me. *That's what I should have been doing instead of playing in the attic,* I told myself, remembering what it was like to be behind in my homework.

Matt had on either the same dark-blue suit I'd seen him in all week, or its twin. I wondered who bought his ties, all conservative stripes in blues and browns.

"I have a few updates," he said, alerting me to the reason I was there. "First, we talked to Leder's wife. We found out she takes sleeping pills occasionally and can't be completely sure she didn't take one on Monday night. So that shakes his alibi a little."

So much for spousal loyalty, I thought, and wondered if Mrs. Leder, whom I'd never met, was looking for a way to get even with her flirting husband. I took notes as Matt continued, reading from the top sheet of a thick file on his desk.

"The Bensens had life insurance, one hundred thousand dollars on each of them, payable to the other."

"Not exactly a fortune these days," I said.

"No, but more than an average secretary like Janice sees in a lump sum very often. Here's what makes it more interesting. We tracked down a phone number on Eric's calendar—turns out he had a meeting scheduled with a divorce lawyer next week."

I shot Matt an *aha* look, but his gaze had wandered to the doorway as we heard an eruption of loud noises. Within a minute Matt's office was filled with balloons, a large flat sheet cake, and about a dozen adults tooting on multicolored paper horns. I was in the middle of Matt's birthday party.

"Surprise!"

"Happy Birthday!"

"Party time!"

Pam, the department secretary, slipped a giant card onto the notebook on my lap and pointed to a place for me to sign. I took the red felt-tip pen she offered and wrote *Gloria Lamerino* in what I hoped was festive script. Pam did her best to introduce me to the reveling crowd while she arranged cups on a tray and poured cola from a giant plastic soft drink bottle.

Matt gave me a helpless look as a tall young policewoman led a chorus of "Happy Birthday" and then read from a Libra horoscope card—*classy, cool, and even-tempered, always in balance, but now's the time to throw back your shoulders and have a ball.*

Matt looked less uncomfortable than I would have been in the same circumstances.

"Let's cut the cake and get rid of that number," he said. Mimicking an evil grin, he picked up a white plastic knife and cut into the center of the cake, slashing through the outline of a speed limit sign with the numbers 55 in black and white icing. I did a quick calculation. He was younger by eight months. Probably a year behind me in school. *Maybe it's a good thing we didn't meet in high school,* I thought, *when the age barrier would have been an issue.* Not that it would have been likely since Matt had gone to Everett High, three or four miles away. In the days before every teenager had a car, we might as well have been across the country from each other.

Matt's birthday cake tasted like a discount supermarket special, but that didn't keep me from eating every crumb on my little white paper plate. The party was over almost as quickly as it had begun and Matt and I were left with the Mylar decorations and a wastebasket overflowing with crumpled napkins and dripping cups. The remains of the cake had been whisked away to the lounge and I felt like the survivor of a heavy but benign windstorm that left the air with the over-sweet smell of cheap frosting.

Matt pinched his nose where his glasses rested, and laughed.

"Wasn't that fun?"

"I'm glad I was invited."

"I'm glad you were, too."

I liked the way he said that. An image of Rose passed before my eyes and I almost invited Matt to dinner, picturing the four of us around Rose's elegant candlelit dining room table. I let the feeling pass.

"Wonderful cake," I said instead, realizing that Rose would have been ashamed of me. Matt laughed again and cleared his throat.

"The divorce lawyer," he said, and I remembered where we'd left off.

"I wonder if Janice knew," I said. "I can't believe Andrea did, or she would have told us."

I paused and rummaged in my briefcase for a pen to give myself a few seconds to debate the wisdom of telling Matt about Annie Lee. Would he consider it meddling? I wondered. Although both Leder and Andrea had mentioned the possibility of a West Coast girlfriend, to my knowledge Matt hadn't pursued it. I plunged in.

"I was talking to a friend in California," I said. "And she reminded me that Eric had the same sort of relationship to another woman out there. A young Korean woman named Annie Lee. Not an affair, exactly, just flirting and 'hanging out,' as Andrea called it."

"Thanks for telling me," Matt said. "I figure anyone still in California is not worth following up at this point. Anyway, none of this necessarily means anything."

"Unless Janice got word of the divorce and was unhappy that Eric would take his degree and run off with someone else. Unhappy enough to murder him," I said, wondering why I was being so pushy.

"Janice is our problem, not yours, since she's not involved

in the technical stuff. It's just as well if you keep out of those lines of inquiry.''

I felt my face heat up and folded my hands like a first grader as I absorbed the mild rebuke. *I have my answer,* I thought. *He* does *consider it meddling.*

''The next item is Connie's alibi,'' Matt said. ''She says she was home alone and made calls to her boyfriend at his hotel in Chicago. The phone logs show nothing after about nine o'clock, so that doesn't help. I'm telling you because you might see something in the computer printout or other lab documents that indicates otherwise. If so, I'd like to know about it.''

Matt looked at me over his glasses. ''I think that's all I have that's new.''

''I'm expecting that some of us will go out for coffee after the wake tonight,'' I said. ''It won't be too hard to get the conversation around to the gas gun data. Something new might emerge.''

''Good,'' Matt said. ''Let's see if we can narrow down what we're looking for from you.''

He took a second file from a basket on the corner of his desk and I noticed the label ''LAMERINO'' along the edge. It was my first glimpse into Matt's organizational style and I didn't know whether to feel flattered to have my own file or slighted because the file was so thin.

''Is that my rap sheet?'' I asked, and immediately regretted the cute remark, blaming the sugar high from the birthday cake for my frivolous mood.

Matt uttered a polite laugh, opened the manila folder, and took out a sheet of paper with handwritten text.

''We'll start with Andrea. We need to know if her work had anything to do with the discrepancy Eric was talking about. Also, how much did the experiment mean to her career, and did it matter to her whether the article got published or not?''

Although heavy-duty crying wasn't proof of innocence, I was tempted to rule out Andrea as Eric's killer. Her alibi seemed good to me, too—home with her two roommates, sleeping in adjacent rooms in a small apartment. But that wasn't what Matt was asking me.

"I doubt that her name would be on the journal paper," I said. "In general a technician just follows instructions from the scientists and engineers. But I'll try to engage her in a technical discussion and see what comes out. Maybe she was applying to grad school and needed this work as a reference."

Matt wrote in his notebook and moved on.

"Next is Connie—" he said. "I still don't quite understand her work, but I'm not ready for a physics lesson right now. Just keep in mind I'll need a little more on that some time."

I made a note to think about an easy explanation of conductivity. Connie would be depending on conductivity measurements for their journal article. As for reputation in the physics community, Connie's was at an important beginning stage.

"Connie talked a lot in California about how the gas gun work was her ticket to a fast rise in high-tech company management," I said, trying to be as objective as possible. "Not that ambition is necessarily a motive for murder."

"Not that it isn't," Matt said. "Jim Guffy looks like a choirboy. And his parents say there's no way he could have left the house without waking them up."

"Jim coaches softball for St. Aidan's in Everett," I said. "He bought a van just so he could take underprivileged kids to ball games."

"But he's a key member of the group and if I remember right, you said his trigger thing was what Eric was raving about the night of the Saint Patrick's Day party."

I made another note, to review the physics of the trigger thing with Matt.

"I know Ralph Leder is high on the list of who profits from Eric's death," Matt said. "We need to know exactly how important these results were to him and this high-tech agreement he's entered into. How much money are we talking about? How far off was the data? Is it something he really could have compensated for in a short time after receiving funding?''

''I have the article describing the negotiations,'' I said. ''I'll look at it more closely and brief you on it.''

''Okay. That's about it,'' he said, closing the LAMERINO folder and putting it back in the basket. He stretched his shoulders back, flexed his fingers, and took a deep breath.

''Which brings me to one final thing,'' he said, folding up his glasses. ''I want to make it clear that in all of this, you're not to take any chances. We don't know for sure, but any one of these people could be a murderer. And they know you're helping us. It doesn't matter if they cry. It doesn't matter if they're your friends. So you must tell me anything that seems suspicious and keep to your role as a purely technical consultant.''

Hearing the emphasis on the words ''must'' and ''anything,'' I wondered if Matt suspected that I was holding something back. I swallowed hard and weighed the merits of telling him about Leder's phone call. I convinced myself it didn't matter right now.

''Are you coming to the wake?'' I asked.

''Yes. Berger's back part time, putting in some hours at the Shirley Avenue substation since he lives near there. He's cleaning up some paperwork on old cases, still in no shape for a regular schedule. I'll see you at the funeral home?''

''I live there,'' I said with a smile, partly from learning that Berger wasn't on the Bensen case yet.

''Right,'' Matt said, returning my smile. He stood up as I gathered my belongings, preparing to leave his office.

''Did you get a chance to look at that printout I gave you?'' he asked.

I felt my face redden as I started my confession.

''Not yet, but I've set aside tomorrow after the funeral. It's something I really need a block of time for. It's very detailed and takes some concentration.''

I was just short of saying ''My dog ate it,'' when Matt waved his hands in a broad sweep in front of his face.

"No problem," he said. "As soon as you can. I know you have a life."

Not really, I thought, *but it's nice of you to think so.* I wanted to continue and tell him how unlike me this was, how I'd gotten bogged down temporarily, how I was overloaded by the emotional interview with Andrea, tension between me and Peter, revisiting my life with Al, and having Eric's dead body in my house.

Matt pulled on the string of a silver balloon with a bright-blue caricature of Lady Justice holding her scales.

"Libra," he said. "Do you think it means that I was born to be in law enforcement?"

His tone was light and I silently thanked him for trying to smooth over my embarrassment at not doing my job.

"What's your sign?" he asked, the singsong rhythm of his voice telling me that he wasn't a fan of astrology. I was relieved at that.

"My birthday's the same as Galileo's," I said, "February fifteenth. I guess I was born to be in science."

Matt laughed and walked with me toward the door. As I brushed some newly found party crumbs from my skirt, I responded to a random thought.

"What's Eric's sign?" I asked.

Matt gave me a quizzical look.

"Andrea said she gave Eric the Einstein figure for his birthday," I said, "and Janice mentioned seeing it in the lab with the action figures around Eric's computer monitor. Janice also said she hadn't been to the lab since the Memorial Day weekend. Maybe . . ."

"Maybe . . ." Matt said, raising his eyebrows and immediately flipping through the file on his desk.

"September twenty-ninth," he said, looking up.

"Enrico Fermi's birthday."

"Whose?"

"Fermi, the Italian and eventually American nuclear scientist—I've been boning up on him for a class and I just happened to remember his birthday. Sorry."

Matt laughed and shook his head as if to ask himself what kind of weird woman he'd hired. I hoped he didn't start suspecting me of Eric's murder.

"In any case, Janice couldn't have seen Einstein in May. Nice going, Gloria."

I wondered how I'd even thought of it and decided that my subconscious mind was working to help me redeem myself for my laziness in other areas.

"It might be nothing," I said.

"It might be something," Matt said.

Chapter Thirteen

Back in my apartment, I went directly to my desk and picked up the computer printout. I hated the idea of black marks in the LAMERINO file. Josephine would not be happy. Whatever her failings, Josephine would never have shirked her responsibilities. Also, I had enough of a competitive spirit to want to solve the case before my designated nemesis and new daddy, George Berger, returned to work.

The format of Eric's printout was the large, wide variety from a continuous feed printer, one long string of attached pages with perforated edges. The alternating white and green rows were supposed to make it easier to distinguish a line of characters from the one just below it, but still it was tough going. Folded up, the stack was about two inches thick. And I wasn't even sure what I was looking for.

I got through all the pages once without a single insight. The only curious thing about the printout was its last line—a series of three characters, the first of which looked like a small triangle, the second the Greek letter mu, and the third an integral sign, ∫. Except for the triangle, the characters were not used anywhere else in the program, neither singly nor as a group—Δμ∫.

Following common practice, Eric used small triangles throughout the program to represent minute differences in the values of a particular quantity. In the gas gun calculations, he used T to represent temperature, and ΔT to represent a small change in temperature. I had no clue, however, how Δμ∫ could represent a small change in μ∫. The Greek letter μ was popular in texts as a representation of parameters that had to do with magnetism, but it hadn't been used at all in Eric's program except for that last line. It was highly unlikely that he was introducing a whole new symbol that far into a calculation.

The third symbol, $\int$, was from calculus, the sign for integration. It was actually an elongated S, standing for "Sum," since an integration in mathematics is a way to add up quantities. The sign would always be followed by what was being summed, such as a function of x. In general, $\int x$ would mean sum all values of x. But it was physically and mathematically meaningless to have an integral sign $\int$ as the last notation, with nothing after it.

I went over the series of characters again and again. Even if Eric had been stopped in the middle of a line, the three characters together didn't make sense in the context of his whole program.

After an hour of getting nowhere, I took a break to make some phone calls. I had a cousin, Mary Ann, a widow in her seventies who lived in Worcester, and I wanted to schedule a weekend with her. Worcester was only about twenty-five miles west of Boston, but I'd already lost the California habit of driving twice that distance just to meet someone for lunch. In my Massachusetts persona I considered twenty-five miles a trip with a postcard-and-slides requirement.

After being in touch with Mary Ann only through Christmas letters and long-distance calls, we were trying to renew family ties. She was the only relative I hadn't completely lost track of.

"I'll bet you're happy to be home," Mary Ann said after we'd picked a mid-November date for my trip.

"Oh, yes, it's wonderful to be back," I said, noting how easily I could skip over my deepest inner conflicts with a blood relative. I'd known right away that Mary Ann wouldn't understand the crazy emotional directions of my life as well as Rose did. And after my cousin's nervous response to my first police contract, I also knew enough not to tell her about my current work on a murder case.

I made an omelet and spread some scrap paper out on the kitchen table next to my plate. I decided to make a simple outline of the conductivity measurements so I could explain them to Matt. I thought it might also be a good way to get a handle on what to look for in the printout.

I wrote notes as if I were preparing a presentation for an overhead projector.

Conductivity:

- The ability of a material to allow electricity to pass through it
- A desirable property for use by utilities and transportation industries
- Has different values at different temperatures and pressures
- Is higher for a metal than for a nonmetal
- Indicates the presence of a metal when a high value is measured

I understood the breakthrough that Leder's team had announced—they claimed they'd been able to measure a conductivity value for hydrogen. From that they inferred that hydrogen existed as a metal, at least for the duration of the measurement, one millionth of a second.

What were the possible ways that the data could be false? I asked myself. It was Jim's trigger signal that switched on the measuring device at just the right time. One possibility was that the trigger signal fired at the wrong time. It might have measured a conductivity that wasn't really for the hydrogen, but for the metal of the container. I made a note to check the conductivity of aluminum, which was what the walls of the target chamber were made of, and compare it to values in the printout.

Another possibility was that the trigger signal fired correctly, and the actual measurement really was low, indicating no metal was present, but the team misread it at first, then had to cover up. Or maybe they didn't misread it, but decided to cover up the low reading. I added a note to check the printout for some numbers that could support any or all of these admittedly wild guesses.

I felt better having accomplished two things: I had a way to explain the significance of the conductivity measurements to Matt and I had at least some leads on what to look for in the printout.

At about six-thirty, Rose called from downstairs and offered to bring up a box of cannoli from Luberto's if I'd make some coffee. She knew I'd never say no to a deal like that. A Luberto's cannoli, with its special creamy custard filling enclosed in a delicate pastry shell, lightly sprinkled with powdered sugar, was my favorite dessert. I wished I hadn't had grocery store birthday cake that afternoon, but it was too late for regrets.

Rose was in a blue-gray dress that nearly matched the color of my sofa. She wore pearls and black pumps, and had tiny onyx studs in her ears. Her mourning outfit. She usually visited with me during wakes when Martha was unavailable to be on call in case office support was needed. This was the first time I'd be attending the wake myself.

"Are you making any progress?" she asked.

I pointed to the papers spread out on my kitchen table, making it unavailable for a pastry session.

"Not a lot," I said. "I'm just getting to the printout."

"That's not what I meant," Rose said. "I'm talking about your love life."

I blew a long sigh into the air above me and considered for a minute telling her that Matt and I had spent the night together and then eloped. I settled on the truth.

"I have no love life," I said, "and I thought you were going to lay off until the case was closed."

"Just asking."

We were seated side by side on the sofa. Rose seemed to have lost her train of thought as she held the cannoli far away from her funeral director outfit. She licked flakes of pastry from her fingers, and I knew I was off the hook.

* * *

Rose and I left the apartment together and walked down to the main parlor a little after seven o'clock.

Walking into the room where Eric was laid out was like walking into the night. I remembered the last few funeral services I'd been to—mostly Protestant ones, where the décor was bright and the spirit was one of new life and resurrection. Was it only Catholics, I wondered, who treated death as a nasty secret, hushed and bleak? Or was it just Galigani's holding on to an old tradition? The piped-in organ music was slow and dreary, as heavy as the scent of many different flowers placed close together in an airless room.

A few more baskets and vases of flowers had arrived since I'd stopped in that afternoon, and Janice was looking through the cards attached to them. When she saw Rose, she walked over to her, holding the white satin-covered guest book between her thumb and index finger as if it needed dusting for fingerprints.

"Do you have another style?" she asked, dropping the book into Rose's open hands. "This seems a little frilly; maybe it's for a woman. I'd prefer something more subtle for a man." Janice was wearing a short black crepe skirt with a matching jacket, topped off by a large chiffon scarf with a black-and-white floral design.

I moved to the side to let Rose handle the crisis.

Straight-backed dark oak chairs with shiny brown and gold fabric seat covers were arranged two deep along the two side walls of the room, creating a wide center aisle in front of the coffin. Eric's parents were sitting in two more comfortable-looking armchairs in the front row to the right of their son's body. They looked much older and smaller than I remembered from the afternoon, and sat holding hands across the arms of their chairs, their shoulders hunched, their mouths in thin lines across deeply wrinkled faces.

I was about to introduce myself, but Janice had finished with Rose, at least for the moment, and met me as I crossed the carpet.

"This is Gloria Lamerino," she said, without looking directly at the couple. "She knew Eric in California."

"These are Eric's parents," she said to me, waving in their direction.

"I'm so sorry," I said to them, with the awkwardness I always feel on such occasions.

"How nice of you to come," Eric's mother said. His father nodded and motioned for me to sit next to him on the one other soft chair in the room as Janice walked away.

Earlier in the day, I'd thought of a few questions I wanted to ask Eric's parents, but once I was in their presence, I lost any inclination to disturb their grief with an interrogation. Instead, I sat next to Mr. Bensen and chatted about how beautiful the flower arrangements were, how Mr. Galigani's men were picking up Eric's grandmother in a brand-new Cadillac, and how Father Tucci was due any minute. Mrs. Bensen sat silently through our conversation, staring in the direction of her son's body and looking old enough herself to be his grandmother.

"Look how far Eric got," Mr. Bensen said. "We had him very late, you know, after we'd practically given up. I'm just a shoemaker, but Eric was always good in school. Even as a little boy he was always doing extra homework."

"Where do you work?" I asked, happy to have a new direction to take the conversation.

"I have a shop on Beach Street, but I'm going to retire now. Eric is my only child, and now he's gone."

I could sense that he had lost interest in life, and before I knew it, I'd asked a question I knew to be inappropriate in such a setting.

"Who would want to kill him?" I asked.

Mr. Bensen turned to me, then looked at Janice who was across the room with other visitors.

"Her," he said.

My eyes must have widened considerably, because Mr. Bensen quickly took my hand.

"Forgive me," he said. "It's just an old man babbling."

I forgave him, but I also wanted to know more. I tried to sound casual as I picked up the thread of his accusation.

"How long were they married?" I asked.

"Eight years. They never should have gotten together in the first place."

I ran the numbers through my head. Eric was thirty-one when he was murdered. That meant he'd married Janice at twenty-three, probably after graduating from college. I knew Eric had been a graduate student for six years, including his year in California, so there were about two years during which he was married to Janice, but not in graduate school.

"Did Eric go to work after college?" I asked Mr. Bensen, keeping my voice low. I thought I might be imposing on Eric's father, but I dismissed the idea as he rambled on. He seemed to be relieved to be able to talk about his son.

"Janice wanted him to work for her father, in the insurance business. Eric tried it but it wasn't for him. I knew that. But Janice pushed him. She thought he could make a lot of money right away like her father."

"So Eric left the company and went back to school?"

"Old man Miller died. And Eric just took the chance to get out. Janice had a fit, but Eric was determined to go back to school. He . . ."

Mr. Bensen started to break down in tears, and I felt an obligation to change the subject. The conversation had proved to be a dead end, anyway, in a manner of speaking. If there was a murder every time a married couple didn't get along, I reminded myself, or one spouse pushed the other into taking a job he or she didn't want, the world would need a lot more homicide detectives.

Several other groups of people were arriving at that moment, and I took advantage of the distraction. I said good-bye to the Bensens and searched the small group of newcomers for a familiar face. Finding none, I took a seat on the opposite side of the room and let my mind wander over Mr. Bensen's nonverbal insinuation that Janice murdered Eric. I convinced myself that he was aware of the strained relationship between his son and daughter-in-law and was merely angry at the thought that Eric might not have died a happily married man.

Sitting in front of Eric's remains, in the presence of his infinitely sad parents, it seemed more crucial than ever to find his murderer and I resolved to give it my all over the weekend.

In the next half hour I was joined by Connie, Jim, Andrea, and Leder, arriving at different times. They were all wearing black somewhere on their person, and so far, with my gray-and-white suit and pewter jewelry, I had the cheeriest outfit in the room. I noticed the guest book in its place on a small wooden stand by the door and wondered how Rose solved Janice Bensen's problem.

There was still no sign of Matt as we sat through a rosary by Father Tucci, the pastor of St. Anthony's. Jim was the only live person besides the priest who held an actual rosary, with dark brown beads and a silver crucifix. I hadn't had a rosary in my hands since I was a child praying for the conversion of Russia, for the souls in purgatory, and for pagan babies. I wondered what happened to my childhood faith. I hadn't consciously abandoned the religion I grew up with, just drifted away from it as I headed west.

As the closing time for the wake approached, I started to think about how to get all the principals together for conversation, but Leder took over.

"You live upstairs, don't you, Gloria?" he asked. As he stood over me, I caught a whiff of an elaborate cologne, reminding me of Peter.

"Yes, it's a wonderful arrangement for now," I said. "My friends own the building and the business."

"Well, why don't we send Jim here to get us a bottle or two, and we can have a fine reunion," he said, taking several bills from his wallet. To my astonishment, I realized he was inviting us all up to my apartment. *What possible motive can he have?* I wondered, dismissing the thought that he was acting out of innocent, if slightly rude, sociability.

Leder stood behind Connie and put his hands on her shoulders.

"See if you can find a bottle of Mondavi for Connie, or anything from one of those Napa Valley wineries," he said, leaning into her ear. Connie rolled her eyes and moved away.

"Maybe we shouldn't invite ourselves," Jim said, still fingering his rosary, part of which hung out of his jacket pocket. He hadn't taken the money Leder was holding out. Connie and Andrea seemed to be echoing Jim's sentiment by giving me questioning looks.

As for me, my second thought after the one about Leder's impure intentions was that my apartment was a mess. I thought about the whole day's worth of dishes in the sink and the books and papers spread out on the table. A voice in my head that sounded like Josephine's told me to ask everyone to wait while I ran up and straightened out. The new voice I was trying to cultivate said no one who matters will judge me by what kind of housekeeper I am.

I looked at the group and smiled. "What a great idea," I said. "It's just up the stairs."

Chapter Fourteen

Jim approached me as if I were his mother and he needed the car keys for the prom.

"I think we should invite Janice and Eric's parents, too, don't you?" he asked.

Evidently Jim felt that an all-inclusive imposition on me was better than one that excluded part of the population. I agreed, grateful that he didn't make a general announcement to the more than two dozen assembled mourners.

Eric's parents declined with grace and Janice accepted with, "I could use a drink." Andrea then bowed out, but not before pulling me aside in the foyer.

"I'm not sure I should tell you this," she said. "But I overheard Dr. Leder on the phone with his wife yesterday. He was arguing with her and I know it was about his alibi for the time of Eric's murder."

"What makes you think that?" I whispered, imitating the low volume of Andrea's words.

"I heard him say something like, 'why the heck did you have to tell them about the sleeping pills?' She's his alibi, isn't she?"

"It doesn't mean he killed Eric."

"No, but it sounded fishy to me. He'd been angry with Eric ever since they came back here. And I know he wanted his wife to lie. He kept saying how she should call the police back and tell them she remembered not taking a pill."

"Why didn't you tell this to the police?"

"It happened way after you and the detective left. It was

late and Dr. Leder probably thought no one else was in the building, but I was in the library right next to his office. The building was so empty the sound carried and before I knew it, I heard the whole conversation.''

Andrea shuffled her feet as she talked, occasionally looking down at the floor as if there were a TelePrompTer on the carpet. Unlike the day of her interview with Matt, her speech came out smoothly, like a dramatic performance given in a stage whisper.

''I thought maybe you could tell the police for me,'' she said, ''since you're helping them.''

''I don't think that's a good idea, Andrea,'' I said, conscious of people not far from us in the parlor, including Leder himself. It might have been my imagination, but I thought he was watching us and lip-reading, and I wasn't anxious to receive another late-night warning call. ''I'm not the police. If you're sure of what you heard and think it's important, you should call Sgt. Gennaro and tell him yourself.''

Andrea didn't look convinced, but it was impossible to continue the discussion as Connie, Leder, and Janice closed in on us. Andrea said good night, and I had no idea if she planned to call Matt, nor even if she was telling the truth in the first place.

A few minutes later, Jim returned from doing his mentor's errand and five of us climbed the stairs and entered my apartment together. I noted without surprise that Jim had included sparkling cider in his selection of drinks, most likely remembering that I don't drink alcohol.

Four people was more company than I'd ever had at one time in my apartment, and I made a mental note to have a dinner party soon with guests of my own choosing.

One look at my cluttered kitchen table was enough to tell even the least observant person what I'd been doing. Evidence of my high-tech snooping was in plain sight: the printout of the gas gun data with red-penciled question marks in the margins, a notebook with my calculations, and the world-famous handbook of physical and chemical measurements, open to the pages on conductivity.

I couldn't have been more embarrassed if all my underwear were strung on a clothesline across the room. Leder's long legs got him to the table before I could get there and clear the trail.

"You've been busy," he said, standing over the table, his hands on his hips where a gun might be holstered if we were in an old western movie. "What's it going to take for you to mind your business, Gloria?"

I wondered how Leder's face could simultaneously support a wide, grinning mouth and pinched, angry eyes. I heard a general shuffling of feet behind us and found myself in the familiar territory of young researchers covering up the unacceptable behavior of their mentor.

"Nice collection of photographs," Jim said.

"Mind if I put on a CD?" Connie asked, and pretty soon Wynton Marsalis was filling the awkward spaces between unconnected bits of conversation.

I'd started to answer Leder with an evasive comment, but changed my mind when I realized that his remarks could be turned into exactly what I'd wanted—a conversation about the gas gun data with at least some of the suspects.

"As a matter of fact this *is* my business," I said. "I've been looking at your printout. One of the things I'm getting paid to do."

Leder's eyes remained pinched together and his nose joined the other angry features of his face, his nostrils growing wider by the second.

"The police said there was no sign of activity on the computer that night," Connie said, before he could collect himself to speak.

"Eventually they were able to pull this up with a lost-and-found utility," I said, pointing to the stack of green and white pages.

"So the killer deleted a file that was on the screen when Eric was murdered?" Jim asked.

''Evidently,'' I said.

By now everyone had gathered around the table and Leder had recovered enough to make one last pitch at putting me in my place.

''Do you really understand our data, Gloria?'' he asked.

Coming from Leder, my name sounded like a little girl's nickname and his question had the lilt of ''can you say your ABCs?''

''I have no problem understanding the data,'' I said, stretching the truth longer than your average rubber band, ''except for these characters at the end.'' I ran my index finger back and forth under the characters $\Delta\mu\int$.

''They're nothing I recognize,'' Connie said.

''Is it some code for the end of the run?'' I asked.

''No, I'd have seen it before if it were,'' she said, while Jim and Leder uttered no's and shook their heads in apparent agreement. ''Besides,'' Connie continued, ''this may be the last page of the printout, but it's not the end of the program. Eric was somewhere in the middle of the program when he typed these characters.''

''So clearly he was interrupted at his keyboard,'' I said.

If anyone was about to give the matter further thought or make a comment, it was swallowed up by Janice's voice.

''Do we have to make this a technical meeting?'' she asked, nearly shouting at us. ''I was under the impression that I was invited to relax with a glass of wine.''

Janice's voice was hoarse and shaky. None of us seemed to have noticed that she'd left the table and taken a place on the sofa. Her chin was in her right hand and she was close to tears.

Connie and Leder appeared stunned. Jim went over and sat next to Janice, and I mentally gave myself the award for the hostess most insensitive to widows.

We stood in silence, made less awkward by the trumpet music, while Janice sobbed on Jim's shoulder. I finally came to and brought her a glass of white wine. I also put a tumbler of water on the coffee table in front of her. *Too little, too late,*

I thought. Josephine knew how to take care of visitors. She'd serve food and drinks with one hand while taking her guests' coats with the other. In a situation like this, with a young woman whose murdered husband lay in a casket below us, Josephine would have attempted to carry the widow to the couch while pouring her drink.

Although it didn't take Janice long to compose herself, the mood for technical talk had passed.

''I'm sorry,'' she said, dabbing at her eyes, ''I guess it's just starting to hit me that Eric is gone.''

Jim continued to sit close to her, giving her alternating drinks of wine and water. *Ever the altar boy,* I thought.

Connie and Leder and I took seats in the living room across from Jim and Janice and talked about friends we had in common on the West Coast. Janice had seen the flower arrangement from some of our California dinner group.

''I'm sure you were responsible for that, Gloria,'' she said. ''Thank you. I never would have thought of calling them.''

''I talk to Elaine Cody regularly,'' I said, ''and it was no trouble for us to contact people. Everyone was truly sorry for your loss.''

''Thank you,'' she said in a soft voice, a great contrast to her usual sharp tones. Janice was showing us a whole new side of herself, subdued and vulnerable. With no apparent thought about the position of her legs or whether a piece of lint had landed on her jacket, she sat on the couch and unceremoniously pulled tissues from the box Jim had found for her.

Connie seemed mellow also, asking about various memories I had of the old Revere. We'd all been, separately, to the big one hundredth birthday celebration held on the beach in July. Revere Beach was the first public beach in the United States and even though the two miles of amusements were gone, the three-mile stretch of sandy beach remained. The city went all out for the anniversary, with games and music, and a fireworks spectacular by the same group that produced the Boston Pops Fourth of July concert every year on the Esplanade in Boston.

"Four of my St. Aidan's boys won second prize in the sand castle competition," Jim said. "I helped them build a scale model of the gas gun, one inch to one foot. It was spectacular. Even had little buttons for control panel lights."

"Did you get any good data from it?" Connie asked, with the widest grin her tiny mouth could handle. "Maybe we can use it."

"Here we go again," Janice said, and we all fell silent for a moment.

We got back to non-lab talk and made a plan to go to Kelly's Roast Beef, at the Point of Pines end of the Boulevard and have a picnic on the beach before it got too cold. *Unless one of us is in jail,* I thought.

After about a half hour, we heard a knock on the door. I thought it might be Rose, who I knew would still be in the building. I was half right. I opened the door to Rose and Matt.

I hoped my face showed only a third of the surprise and pleasure I felt. Matt was wearing a different suit, a darker blue, newly pressed. He looked newly shaven, too, and had as comfortable an expression as if his presence were expected.

Rose spoke up to set everything thing straight.

"Matt came just as we were closing up," she said. "He saw the lights and all the cars and thought we might still be here. He was right." At this last phrase, she swept her arms across the room to encompass the party, and looked as if she might take a bow.

Matt greeted everyone and went over to Janice. *He knows how to treat a victim,* I thought.

Rose took over as hostess, refilling glasses and serving Matt sparkling cider at his request. I guessed he considered himself on duty although I had no reason to believe he drank otherwise.

My first apartment party didn't last much longer, ending with our making plans for getting to St. Anthony's for Eric's funeral service the next morning.

Leder, Connie, Janice, and Jim left at the same time. I heard Jim offer to drive Janice home, but she said she was fine. Rose reminded her that a limousine would pick her up in the morning. I may have imagined it, but I thought I heard Connie utter a soft but firm "no thank you" to Leder.

Matt had stayed behind and Rose was talking to me with her face, her dark eyes darting from me to Matt to the door. I understood her as only friends do, and talked back. The gist of the eye-to-eye conversation was Rose's noting how Matt was still here and wanted to be alone with me, and my answering *no, that's not it and please don't go.*

Rose ignored my unspoken but clear request, and excused herself.

"Well, I have a busy morning," she said. "And Frank isn't feeling that well, so I'll be going."

I walked her to the door, keeping my eyes and jaw busy telling Rose what I thought of her behavior. Matt was standing in the living room, his hands in his jacket pockets. He had abandoned his pleasant look for a more serious one. I offered him more cider.

"No, thanks," he said. "If you don't mind, I'm going to look around."

"You want a tour?" I asked, not quite ready for this request.

"You can call it that," he said, smiling in a way that made me feel foolish. Evidently I was missing some obvious point.

"You've just had the prime suspects in a murder investigation in your home," he said. "Not a good idea. I couldn't believe it when Rose told me you were entertaining them up here. I waited downstairs to give you some time, but that doesn't mean I approve."

"It wasn't my idea," I said. "Leder suggested it. And I thought you agreed it would be good if I could have a conversation with them tonight."

I heard my feelings of anger and dismay coming through as I stood with my arms straight down by my side and my voice came out high and whiny. I came within seconds of giving in to my desire to stamp my feet.

"At a restaurant," he said, still with the tone of a parent

displeased with his daughter's choice of friends. ''Even a bar. In a public place. Not in your home.''

He had moved to the kitchen and was looking at my cabinets, on top of my refrigerator, under the sink. He picked up my phone receiver, then replaced it when he heard a dial tone. He walked toward my bedroom, looked in the closet and under the bed, out the window and down at the street. I could hear cars starting up and pulling away, but they didn't distract me from trying to figure out what Matt was doing.

''What are you looking for?'' I asked. My voice was small and weak as I followed him around my apartment.

''I'm doing a sweep,'' he said, ''making sure you have no surprises tonight. What's in here?''

Matt had walked through my bedroom, past my exercise bicycle to the small hallway. He looked up at the trapdoor with a questioning look.

''Isn't that funny,'' I said, trying to restore normalcy to this strange turn of events. ''This corridor seems to have no purpose except to lead to the attic.''

Matt didn't respond. He pulled the ladder to the trapdoor, hooked it to the edge, and started climbing.

''No one went up there,'' I said. ''No one left the kitchen and living room area. And even if they did . . .''

''No one that you saw.''

''Do you think someone planted a bomb or something?''

''It's not my job to guess, just to cover all bases.''

His voice was cold and patronizing, and I felt like a whipped child. I stood in the hallway, my arms across my chest, and listened to Matt's footsteps across the length of the attic floor. When he came down a few minutes later I saw small piles of dust on his shoes and on the shoulders of his dark jacket. *This can't get much worse,* I thought.

He brushed himself off.

''I'm sorry,'' I said, and reached out to help him. I pulled my hand back halfway to his shoulder when I saw his gaze. I felt the way I did when I was little and didn't understand why Josephine was screaming at me. I thought I'd built up resistance over the years to the feeling of helplessness when someone expressed disapproval of me, but at that moment in the presence of Matt's displeasure, my adult resources failed me.

We walked back through the bedroom and living room toward the door without speaking.

Matt took a business card from his inside pocket, wrote on it, and handed it to me. He checked the lock on the door.

"If you see or hear or so much as feel anything strange, call me at that number," he said, and walked out.

Chapter Fifteen

Eric's murder was not good for my health, I decided. In the past week, I'd been through more emotional upheavals and sleepless nights than my average year since Al's fatal car crash.

I'd worked hard all my adult life to overcome feelings of inadequacy instilled in me from birth. When you grow up afraid of your mother, there's not much hope of facing the world with confidence. You end up willing to do anything to please people, even bus drivers or waiters you'll never see again.

Not that Josephine ever laid a hand on me. She kept control through intimidation and verbal abuse, making it clear that my birth was an accident she wasn't happy about. It was a long time before I realized that I wasn't the cause of her miserable life—the villain was the utter lack of opportunity for an intelligent but poor immigrant woman at the beginning of the twentieth century.

I kept reminding myself of all the good that came from her threats. I got all As in high school because I sincerely thought she'd kill me if I didn't. I went to college for the same reason. Josephine was convinced that education was the way out of the kind of life she had. How she'd become enlightened about that, I'd never know.

I often had arguments with myself about the consequences of Josephine's domination. Would I rather be a self-confident housewife who never left her kitchen or a professional scientist afraid of her own shadow?

I made a different choice each time, depending on my mood. Once in a while I made a resolution to be a professional scientist not afraid of her own shadow. On that Saturday morning after Matt's scolding, I was just about to make a new decision when the phone rang.

It was nine A.M. and Peter was calling for one last check on my schedule for the evening. He'd bought tickets for the Wonderland dinner dance anyway, since it was for charity, and wondered if I'd be able to fit it in.

"Rose and Frank are going," he said, throwing in a carrot. "And there's room at their table."

Here was Peter offering me an easy way out. I didn't have to work very hard to please him—he already liked me. No fear of rejection to worry about. Just a nice pleasant relationship with clear rules. I could hardly remember why it hadn't worked with Peter during our first lifetime together.

"What time?" I asked.

"Cocktails at six," he said. "I'll pick you up at five-thirty. But if that's too early for you, we can go later. Dinner's at seven-thirty."

I heard the surprise and pleasure in Peter's voice and mentally pictured him tearing up the other nine points he'd written out to convince me to go with him. It felt good to please someone.

"Five-thirty's fine," I said.

"Are you awake?" Peter asked.

"Am I awake? Yes, why?"

"Well, I guess I'll call you at this time more often."

"Don't press your luck," I said, and heard his laugh trail away as we hung up. *Perfect,* I thought. No time for any other decisions for a while, except what to wear to a dinner-dance.

I was hanging my black knit dress on the shower rod for a quick amateur steaming when I heard the intercom buzzer and Rose's voice.

"So, I assume last night didn't go so well?" she said.

"What do you mean?"

I couldn't believe Rose heard what had gone on after she left. Matt hadn't actually screamed at me the way Josephine used to.

"Well, since Peter just called to say we're on for tonight, I guess your evening with the prince of detectives was less than a grand slam."

Rose never did well with metaphors, but I got her meaning.

"You don't know the half of it."

"I'm all ears."

"I'm still not dressed for church," I said. "Later."

"I can hardly wait. See you."

What would I do without Rose? I wondered. There was no one else like her in my life, maybe because we knew each other as young girls, dressing alike and talking about our hair and every little thing that matters when you're ten or eleven years old. I almost regretted the time away from her, but it didn't seem to have affected our closeness.

I clicked on my weather radio and looked out the window at the same time. The consensus seemed to be rain all day. I was still like a newcomer to New England weather and enjoyed the sound and feel of rain. Years of near-drought conditions can do that. Of course, I had to admit it had been nice to plan outdoor events for any day between Easter and Thanksgiving and be ninety percent sure it wouldn't rain.

For the funeral I settled on a long wide skirt and high leather boots, both a deep gray, hoping I didn't look too much like a cowgirl. To give the outfit a decidedly metropolitan slant I pinned a stylized silver initial *G* in a modern setting to my sweater. I got my gray raincoat and matching hat from the hall closet and headed for the church.

It had taken me a while to determine my mode of transportation for the funeral. I didn't like either image of myself in Eric's funeral procession—behind the wheel of an otherwise empty black Cadillac or high up on the seat of the burgundy four-wheel-drive I still hadn't gotten rid of. My compromise plan was to walk the short distance to St. Anthony's and then ride with someone else to the cemetery.

* * *

Robert Galigani, looking like a younger version of Frank, led Janice and Eric's parents past about fifty mourners, to the front row of the church. After seeing the rosary in Eric's hand, I expected a full-blown funeral mass but there was only a brief service, and I had the idle thought that it was a waste of the great cathedral-like size and atmosphere of St. Anthony's not to have a high mass with all the trimmings.

In the lobby of the church I approached Jim Guffy and asked if I could ride with him to Holy Family Burial Grounds.

"Sure," he said, "I get it."

I had no idea what he meant, but focused on the fact that I had a ride to the cemetery. In the parking lot, Jim's vehicle was easy to spot, a high-riding black minivan with overlapping bumper stickers competing for space. Antidrug slogans, Christian fishlike symbols, and a half-dozen cartoon mascots for neighborhood sports teams covered the back bumper and spare tire cover.

After clearing out duffel bags and balls of various sizes and stitching patterns, and adding a yellow and black funeral sign to his collection, Jim helped me up onto the passenger seat. I sat just below a swinging St. Christopher medal.

It wouldn't have occurred to me to interrogate Jim on the long slow ride to the cemetery, but his opening remarks indicated that he had a different idea.

"Are you going to ask me about Eric?"

"What do you mean?"

"I know you're working on the case with the police, so I figure you're here to ask me some questions."

"Well, as a matter of fact, I really did just need a ride, Jim. I didn't think my Jeep would fit in with a funeral procession."

"I certainly had no respect for Eric, if that's what you want to know," Jim said, apparently intent on treating me like an investigating officer. "You have to love the sinner but not the sins. I'm offering special prayers for his soul."

I straightened up on my seat and turned to look at Jim, as far as my seat belt would allow. His face had a pinched look, his forehead marked with frown lines, his chin thrust out toward the steering wheel. As Jim talked on, using phrases that reminded me of catechism classes, like "mortal sin," "state of grace," and "submission to the will of God," I was struck as much by his demeanor as his words. His attitude was angry and self-righteous, markedly different from the low-key temperament he'd maintained even during our dinnertime debates in California.

As I sat in Jim's van, I had no desire to enter into a discussion. The best I could think of was what I considered a neutral statement.

"No one deserves to be murdered," I said.

Jim helped me out of the van and we stood next to each other during the brief service around Eric's closed casket, displayed next to a mound of dirt and flowers. Holy Family was on Washington Avenue, less than a mile from Charger Street, and the three-story gas gun building where Eric was murdered was visible through the heavy atmosphere.

Although the rain had dwindled to a light mist, we stood under enormous black umbrellas provided by Galigani's. As I watched tiny black sparrows take cover in the bushes and trees of the cemetery, I felt sad for Eric's parents and sad that I hadn't done as much as I should have to find his murderer.

I also couldn't get Jim's tirade out of my head, and I wondered if his anger was the kind that resulted in murder.

Following a plan laid down by the group in my living room the night before, we went from the cemetery to a coffee shop on Route 1. Jim had been quiet on the second lap of our trip, possibly feeling that his preaching was falling on deaf ears.

"Thanks for inviting me," I heard Andrea say to Jim as we were getting into a red leatherlike booth. "It makes me feel part of things to be here."

Andrea's eyes were red and puffy. She stuffed tissues into the pocket of her rain poncho and drew a chair up to the end of the table. I wondered if she called Matt to tell him her story about Leder's phone call to his wife. I had no intention of asking her, however, not wanting to encourage her to think of me as an accessory to the information. The other four of us sat in pairs across from one another, Connie and Leder on one side, thanks to aggressive posturing by Leder, and Jim and I on the other.

"We'll all miss him," Jim said, sounding once again like the facilitator we all knew and loved.

For the second time in less than twenty-four hours, the principal suspects in Eric's murder were eating and drinking together, except that this time it was breakfast, and we had Andrea instead of Janice. It occurred to me that Eric's death had brought this group together in a way that probably wouldn't have happened if he'd lived. Once we'd all arrived back in the Boston area, our dinner meetings ended. I'd had a brief encounter with Jim at a science education meeting, and we talked about getting together again, but did nothing about it. Just like many families, I realized, coming together for disasters.

The restaurant had a vaguely familiar feel to it, like the ones I'd tried to avoid on my way across the country. The menus were old and sticky and the waitress' hands seemed to be the same. I ordered coffee and an English muffin.

"I didn't see the detective at the funeral," Leder said, looking at me. "Maybe he had a rough night."

I focused on the glass of water in front of me as the rest of the group went into cover-up mode, as they had the night before.

"Let's hope he's busy tracking a killer," Connie said.

"I saw some guys at the back of the church who looked like cops to me," Jim said.

The things we endure to get a degree, I thought, and silently thanked my own mentor at the University of California for his pleasant and dignified manner.

I was wrestling with the idea of bringing up the printout or the trigger signal or the conductivity measurements, anything to get on the track of the gas gun work. Matt's behavior the night before seemed to have cramped my style. I half expected him to burst into the restaurant and yell at me for sitting in the same booth with the suspects.

While I was debating with myself, the conversation went on without me.

"Did Dominic have a good time?" Andrea asked Connie.

"Great," Connie said. "It was nice to have him while Bill was away. We had some good long talks."

Jim, ever vigilant to include everyone, turned to me and asked, "Did you know Connie has a twin brother, Dominic?"

"How interesting. No, I didn't," I said.

Jim continued after the ancient waitress had filled our mugs with coffee.

"He's a big-shot chemist for a pharmaceutical company," Jim said. "On the high-paying end of technology."

"Does he still live in Connecticut?" Andrea asked. "It's Groton, isn't it, where the big R&D facility is?"

"Yes," Connie said in a tiny, clipped voice, clearly not wanting to pursue the topic.

If Connie hadn't looked at me at that moment, I might have missed the significance of the information—Connie had a visitor from Connecticut in the time frame of Eric's murder. She and I were sitting directly opposite each other, and I caught her glance, sharp and brief, and speaking volumes.

"They're pretty different from each other," Jim said.

"I hear they both drive red cars, though," I said.

"I thought you didn't know about him."

"Just guessing."

Connie lowered her eyes and let out a long, deep breath. My comment drew enough innocent laughter from the others to cover her reaction. Since no one else had seen the police report, I guessed that they didn't know about the red Corvette with Connecticut plates in the parking lot on the night of Eric's murder.

I tried to process the picture of Connie driving her brother's car to the lab on Tuesday night, shooting Eric in cold blood, then going back to finish her homework for her management class.

We stayed at the table for another twenty minutes, discussing the Red Sox, the Boston Symphony, and other topics irrelevant to the murder. I'd decided that I'd already learned enough for one meal and didn't bring up the experiment.

Connie picked at her omelet, and seemed to have no energy, not even to ward off Leder's arm, which he'd rested along the back of the booth behind her.

Jim took on the job of figuring out the parts of the check.

As we moved out of the booth, Connie said, "Jim, I have to do an errand near the church, so why don't I drop Gloria off?"

It didn't dawn on me until I was buckled into Connie's car that if the scenario I'd just worked out was true, Connie could make me her next victim. What would Matt say about this, I wondered?

We drove in silence until we were on the highway headed south toward Revere.

Connie kept both hands on the wheel and turned to me.

"I guess I should go to the police," she said.

"I guess you should."

"My car was out of oil. You can ask Bill. This Beemer is a 'seventy-three on its last legs. It needs oil every week," Connie said, slamming her hand on the steering wheel. "So I took Dominic's Corvette. I wasn't trying to hide anything. But after what happened, I was afraid to admit I was there."

"What were you doing at the lab at midnight?"

I'm cross-examining a murder suspect, I thought, *while she's at the wheel of a car doing sixty-five miles an hour.* I might have questioned my sanity except that I didn't believe Connie killed Eric. *She isn't acting like a murderer,* I told myself, as if I had any reason to know how a murderer acts.

Connie's fingers were gripping the wheel, her eyes focused on the road. Once or twice I felt a lurching as she changed lanes, but for the most part, she appeared in control.

"I knew Eric was thinking of retracting the journal article," she said. "I went there to talk him out of it. Eric worked late a lot, so at ten-thirty I decided to take a ride over to the lab and see if he was there. It was better than trying to talk to him during the day with everyone around. I figured if I could catch him off-guard, he might listen to reason. I got there about eleven. I stayed and did some work until a little after one, and when he didn't show up I left.''

''So there is something wrong with your data?''

''Yes, I'll show you. I'll show the police. I've had it with trying to cover it. Leder's going to get us all in trouble.''

I kept my eyes on her, as if my surveillance could prevent any dangerous moves on her part. A steak house that was famous in the area, several motels, and fast-food restaurants whizzed by behind Connie's profile.

Connie turned her eyes back to me.

''I didn't kill him,'' she said.

I remembered Thursday's interview with Andrea.

''You're the second person who's told me that,'' I said.

Chapter Sixteen

As Connie pulled up at Galigani's, I remembered the fuss Matt had made about potential murderers in my apartment. I told myself that this was different—only one person instead of four, and she was tiny. With this sloppy reasoning at the front of my brain, I brought Connie into my home.

We sat at my kitchen table, the computer sheets spread out in front of us, a paper road paved with alpha-numeric characters, while Connie explained the cover-up around the conductivity measurements.

"Here's the real measurement," she said, marking several lines with a red pencil. "We got exactly the kind of negligible number you'd expect for a gas, far from the number we would have gotten if we'd really made a metal."

She'd taken off her navy-blue suit jacket and her cropped knit top showed off her trim form. Connie had the figure of a teenager, although not me as a teenager. I always smiled when my women friends referred to getting back their "girlhood figures." Mine was nothing to go back to. Even at fifteen, I was uncomfortable tucking a blouse into my skirt, and at fifty-five I didn't own a single belt.

Connie looked more like the cheerleaders I'd envied in high school. I realized that she probably had to work against that image to get as far as she had in a male-dominated field. One more reason for her to wear extra-large T-shirts and a lab coat on the job. And to cultivate an abrasive personality, I added, giving her the benefit of the doubt for a moment.

Connie pointed to a line that ended with EX10-26, their

computer's shorthand for a number that represents a tiny fraction of a unit. I was already planning how I'd explain the numbers to Matt—the minus sign between the 10 and the 26 represented an infinitesimally small fraction, one so small that there wasn't a name for it like hundredth or even billionth of a unit. In other words, Connie's team had observed virtually no conductivity for the hydrogen in the target chamber.

"Here's where we fudged it," she said, moving the pencil down a few lines, her jaw and shoulders more relaxed than her usual posture. She underlined an entry with a string of at least a dozen characters that ended with EX10+32. This number, added to the real number, put the measurement in the correct range for a metal.

"We just inserted these extra lines into the program. There's almost zero chance that anyone would notice."

Listening to Connie's voice, you'd never guess she was explaining how she and her colleagues had committed fraud in an attempt to obtain a great deal of money from an unsuspecting industrial partner. I guessed her composure was due to her relief at finally being able to tell the truth.

I wasn't sure how much tutoring Matt would need to understand this, but I thought of making the analogy of being twenty-six dollars in debt in your checkbook, then just writing in a deposit of thirty-two dollars, with no cash to back it up, making it seem you were six dollars in the black. In the same way, adding EX10−26 to EX10+32, gave the net result of EX10+6. For reference I'd explain to Matt that pure copper metal had about that same conductivity, and that's why the team chose 32 as the fudge factor.

Once I understood the technical aspects of the cover-up, which I'd never have been able to figure out on my own, I picked up my cross-examination of Connie. It was hard for me not to show the anger I felt at this betrayal of my profession, but I remained placid while I still needed more information from her.

"Who else knew about this?" I asked.

"Leder, of course. It was his idea, but Eric and I went along with it. We rationalized that by the time the new facility was built, we would have worked out the problem, and no one would be the loser.''

Connie had put the pencil down and sat back in her chair. She took a deep breath and accepted my offer of coffee. I put out a plate of white and yellow cheeses leftover from the night before and she had several slices. Since I'd apparently ruined her breakfast, I felt an obligation to feed her. I ignored what I thought might be Matt's response if he knew I was entertaining an admitted fraud and possible murderer as if she were my cousin Mary Ann from Worcester.

''So Jim's electronic trigger worked as it was supposed to?'' I asked.

''Yes. As drunk as he was, Eric didn't give anything away at Jim's party. If anyone checked the trigger signal, everything would be in order. I doubt that Jim knows what we did. He's not that involved in the computations, and he's the last one we'd tell if we didn't have to. He'd be running off to confession.''

I winced at her disregard of Jim's integrity, but I let it slide. First, I wasn't through with her, and second, just in case this physicist who looked like a homecoming queen was really a killer.

''I'll bet it ruined the party for Leder,'' I said.

''You bet. He was ticked at Eric. He called a meeting of anyone who might be worried, and smoothed everything over. He's a master at that.''

''So, basically, Leder, Eric, and you are the only partners in this fraudulent scheme?''

Connie broke down in tears, maybe at my choice of words. I should have seen it coming, but I'd been focusing on her answers to my questions. I wished I had current statistics on how crying related to innocence or guilt. So far, all the women involved in this investigation had gotten choked up or cried, including me. If all the women were innocent and Jim was a saint, that left Leder as the only remaining suspect. I breathed deeply and decided it might be time to tell Matt about Leder's phone call to me.

I led Connie over to the sofa, to the same spot where Jim had comforted Janice the night before. We talked for a while about our careers, how difficult it was to be one of so few women in physics. When I'd received my Ph.D. in 1968, women made up two to three percent of that population. More than twenty-five years later, the figure had mushroomed to four to six percent. It still wasn't crowded in the ladies' rooms of the nation's physics buildings.

"I know that doesn't justify doing what I did to succeed," she said. "But Leder has all this power over us. And he made it sound all right. We're a good team and we can make a contribution."

"What you've contributed so far is the worst thing for science as far as I'm concerned," I said, forgetting the wisdom of being cautious until we knew for sure who killed Eric. "Some people love to think that scientists cheat and make up data to get money. And you've helped them believe they're right."

My sermon was more for myself than for Connie. I'd always erred in the opposite direction, wanting to think that only the purest motives drove research scientists. It was hard for me to take this undeniable evidence to the contrary. The fact that the greed of a scientist might have led to a murder made the situation even more horrible for me.

"I know, I know," Connie said, standing up and straightening her tiny skirt. "I'm going to talk to Sgt. Gennaro. Will you come with me?"

"Yes," I said. "I'd like to be there."

I called Matt's pager number and was surprised to reach him at his office on a Saturday afternoon. I explained that Connie had some information to give him about the printout, leaving out the part about who owned the Corvette in the parking lot. I wasn't anxious to alert him further that Connie might be the murderer. He wasn't easy to manipulate, however.

"Is Connie there in your home right now?" he asked, his voice expressing the displeasure that I was starting to get used to.

"Yes," I said in a soft voice that I hoped Connie didn't hear. "Everything's fine. We'll be there shortly if that's all right."

"Hold on," he said, leaving me with a brief interlude of Lawrence Welk-like music. He was back on the line a few seconds later.

"There's a cruiser at Broadway and Tapley Avenue," Matt said. "He'll pick you up in less than five minutes. Be at the curb. And make sure Connie knows the plan. Is that clear?"

"Yes, it's clear," I said, feeling once more at his mercy.

I used a significantly different tone when I told Connie that we were being escorted to the police station. I tried to make it sound as though the department routinely provided taxi service as a courtesy to its friends.

Before we left the apartment for our curbside rendezvous with the police car, I remembered another question and picked up Eric's computer printout. I thought Connie might be more willing to share information than she had been the night before.

"What about these characters at the bottom. Do they have anything to do with the false conductivity equations or measurements?" I asked her.

"I still have no idea what those are," she said, shrugging her petite shoulders. "They have nothing to do with our data."

As she finished her sentence, we heard the police car pull up. I was grateful that at least there was no siren and flashing lights.

In Matt's office, Connie told him first about taking her brother's car and being at the lab on Monday evening until one in the morning, apparently thinking that was the most incriminating aspect of her story.

I took the printout from my briefcase and Connie showed Matt the lines that were significant to the falsified data. Her voice was higher than usual and she twisted her hair around her fingers like a schoolgirl. I didn't interrupt while she explained the fudge factor to Matt in terms that I knew were too technical for him.

I was still unhappy that she didn't seem to appreciate the gravity of what she'd done with physics research data. This was different from working backward to get the right answer for the momentum of a ball bearing in a freshman physics lab, I wanted to tell her, but I decided not to speak until I was spoken to.

A young Asian man in beige slacks and sports jacket came to the door and was introduced as Detective Wu. I pictured him living on Shirley Avenue near where Steiner's Deli used to be.

''Dr. Provenza, I'm going to ask you to step outside with Detective Wu and give him a new statement. And I'll want to see you again before you leave.''

I stood up, but Matt motioned for me to sit down and I did, clutching my briefcase all the while, feeling like an uptight puppet. I was not looking forward to this conversation. I changed my mind about keeping silent.

''Do you think she killed Eric?'' I asked.

''Let's talk about some other things,'' he said. ''Why don't you tell me how all this came about.''

I started with the revelation about Connie's brother, then moved on to the session in my apartment with the printout. I felt an enormous letdown when Matt told me they'd already closed in on identifying the car. The police had been back questioning physics department personnel, and of course many people mentioned Connie's twin brother from Groton.

''This, on the other hand, I don't get,'' he said, pointing to the printout. Finally I saw the hint of a smile and relaxed. I launched into my explanation of Connie's data and the way they'd faked it, using the checkbook analogy I'd worked out in my apartment.

''Why do metals conduct more electricity than other materials?''

''It's the way the electrons are arranged in a metal—they're more free to move.''

''And these moving electrons produce electricity?''

''Actually, these moving electrons *are* electricity—that is, we call moving electrons 'electricity.' It may sound like only semantics, but it's an important distinction in understanding how physicists develop their jargon.''

For a few minutes, I had a good time, feeling useful and appreciated. Matt asked a few more questions and thanked me, but didn't let me get away without another warning speech.

''I don't know what to do with you,'' he said. ''You apparently are not going to follow my advice, so I'm going to have to make it stronger. This is not a suggestion. You're not to operate on your own in this investigation. It's a violation of your contract for one thing, and extremely foolish, for another. If you see or hear anything you think is significant, you don't handle it yourself. You call me.''

Matt leaned toward me as he talked, emphasizing certain words by tapping his hands on his desk blotter.

''I have something else to tell you,'' I said. ''Not exactly what we're talking about but I should have told you before.''

He leaned forward a few more inches and opened his eyes wide. He tilted his head and tightened his jaw. I was sorry I mentioned it, but there was no turning back. I told him about Leder's phone call on Wednesday night, but not the gossip from Andrea's alleged eavesdropping incident, so I felt only partly cleansed, as if I'd been to confession and held back a sin.

He let out a loud breath, but seemed to take it better than I thought he would. If he felt he'd intimidated me enough, he was right.

''Okay,'' he said, ''thank you. Is there anything else?''

''Yes,'' I said. I flipped over the computer printout so the last lines of the stack were on top. ''There are three symbols at the end of the program that seem out of place.''

Chapter Seventeen

I left the station with the same officer who'd picked Connie and me up earlier in the evening. As I stepped into the white cruiser I noted the red script along the bottom of the back door. *Revere Pride*, it read, and I wondered if whoever created the slogan meant the cars, the officers, or the special escort service for naive amateur detectives.

Connie's car was not in front of Galigani's where I'd last seen it, so I assumed she was finished before I was. *Or else they've put her in jail and impounded her car,* I thought. In any case, I was ready to admit to myself that it wasn't my problem. My problem was to get ready for a double date with Peter and Rose and Frank.

As I entered the front door of Galigani's, I saw Rose standing on the second-floor landing, her hands on her hips, her eyes full of energy. When I reached her level, she pulled me into her office.

"I can't stand it, Gloria. You have to tell me what's going on."

"What do you mean?" I asked.

Neither of us could get much farther without a burst of laughter.

We each took one of the upholstered chairs in front of her desk. Rose was still in her funeral garb, but I knew she wouldn't be here if she didn't already have a smashing outfit laid out on her bed for our evening of dinner and dancing.

"A cruiser picks you up and drops you off. What's that

about? And what happened last night with Matt? How come you're going out with Peter?"

"More important," I said, "how did you handle the guest book crisis with Janice Bensen?"

She looked as if she'd lose her breath if I didn't satisfy her curiosity. But she played along for another minute.

"I told her we'd use it as is for the evening, and then later we'd add a cover on top of the white linen that she thinks is too feminine. She can have any color of her choice."

"Brilliant," I said, patting her knee.

She folded her hands on her lap and looked at me as if to remind me that she'd earned the right to some information. I knew it was my turn. I told her why Matt stayed behind and she seemed as disappointed as I was that it was for less-than-romantic reasons.

"He was really upset when I told him you had Eric's wife and friends up here," Rose said. "I think he cares a lot about you."

"He doesn't care about me in particular, Rose. He just doesn't want a civilian employee dead on his watch."

"You're pouting, Josephine," Rose said, using her old trick of calling me by my mother's name whenever she detected a regression to my childhood training.

"Okay, never mind. Let's move on to the police escort," I said.

I explained that the cruisers were due to what I thought was Matt's paranoia about my having Connie in my apartment once I knew she'd been at the crime scene on the night of the murder. To my surprise, Rose took his side.

"I never thought of that risk," she said, frowning as she did when she was serious. "He's right. Excitement is one thing, but you can't be putting yourself in danger."

"Well, there won't be any more excitement or danger. My job is almost over."

"You mean they're going to arrest one of the scientists?"

"Not necessarily, but there's not much more for me to do."

We looked at the clock, a mahogany heirloom like Rose's

desk. Even though most clients never saw Rose's office, it was beautifully furnished with antiques from her family.

"Well, I've got work to do," she said, leaning over to show me the roots of her chemically enhanced dark hair. We left her office together.

As soon as I closed my own apartment door behind me, I realized that I'd left my briefcase in Rose's office. I grimaced in annoyance since I'd wanted one more look at my notes. Somewhere I had a key to the second-floor rooms, but I'd never used it and couldn't remember where it was.

Finally I decided not to bother, that a better idea was to fill my tub with water and lavender foam from Crabtree & Evelyn and forget about the investigation. I couldn't give it up completely, however, so before I got in to soak I put a notebook and pencil on the small white wicker stool next to the tub, just in case I had a brilliant insight.

I wondered how Leder and Connie would work out the debt they owed the scientific community. My opinion of Leder was low enough that I thought he might divert all the blame to Connie. As project leader he could take the high ground and say that he merely allowed his name to be used on the research papers of his underlings and had no knowledge of the fraud. In any case they'd have to retract their paper and face the consequences in front of a review board of their peers.

Although the technical mystery of the hydrogen data was solved, I still had a lot of questions. Was what the scientists had done enough to think of them as murderers? If so, who—Connie or Leder or both? It wasn't as if fudged data were the only motive for killing Eric.

I mentally reviewed my notes, which were as clear in my head as they were on paper. Andrea seemed eager to cast suspicion on Leder. At first I thought she might have made up the whole story about Leder's call to his wife, but how else would she have known about the sleeping pills or what Leder and his wife told the police?

There was still Andrea's own motive to think about, and

Janice's. Surely jealousy and domestic discord were still more popular motives for murder than damage to scientific reputations. And for all his holy image, I couldn't rule out Jim as a possibility.

Even though it was none of my business, I wished Matt would share more of his thinking on procedural matters with me. I wondered if he had followed up on the discrepancy in Janice's statement that she hadn't been to the lab since Memorial Day. I also wondered if Janice knew about Eric's scheduled meeting with the divorce lawyer or that he allegedly had a girlfriend in California.

I knew my assignment was almost over—technically, the only thing left for me to do was figure out what if anything the strange characters on the printout meant. I stretched a dripping arm over to the stool, picked up the pencil, and wrote $\Delta\mu\int$ on my notepad. I stared at it for a while, then closed my eyes as the watery letters became blurry and illegible.

As I dressed, I tried to shift my thoughts from Matt to Peter. My black knit dress had come back to life after its morning steam bath. I looked in the bathroom mirror and felt I was as presentable as I could hope to be, after adding a long strand of faux pearls, drop pearl earrings, and the highest heels I owned, two inches, in black patent leather. No pin for this outfit.

Peter knocked on my door at exactly five-thirty, wearing the brightest smile and the most sharply pressed suit I'd ever seen. His black wing tips were as polished as many a lens I've seen on an optical bench. He took my hand and stepped back to arm's length.

"Gloria," he said, slipping a corsage with tiny red tea roses on my wrist. He gave me a hug like the ones I've seen baseball players give a batter as he crosses home plate. I wondered if he was congratulating me on my outfit or himself on talking me into this date.

I offered him wine leftover from the stock Leder had supplied, but he refused.

"I'm driving," he said. "And we need to pick up Rose and Frank in fifteen minutes."

When Peter said fifteen minutes, he meant exactly fifteen minutes. I expected him to have worked out the evening's schedule for a smooth operation, leaving nothing to chance. My suspicions were confirmed as I entered his dark blue Buick and smelled the unmistakable odor of a brand-new cedar air freshener tree.

The Galigani home was across town and up a hill on Adams Street. In the old days Revere Memorial Hospital was around the corner from them, on Proctor Avenue. Josephine had spent the last twenty-four hours of her life in that hospital, and my father had spent his last days there many years later. Rose had told me that in the late seventies the hospital was converted to a multilevel nursing home. I looked at the tall, imposing building, visible from Rose and Frank's driveway, and was glad I didn't have time to dwell on memories of my parents' deaths.

As I guessed, except for being nearly a foot shorter, Frank met the standard Peter had set for sharpness. And Rose's outfit was smashing—a calf-length electric-blue chiffon, with matching high-heeled sandals. I felt dowdy in their company, but that was nothing new.

"How's the investigation coming?" Frank asked, earning himself disgusted looks from his wife and Peter.

"Thanks for asking," I said, smiling at Frank. "I'll tell you later."

We drove together to the Wonderland Ballroom, a one-story yellow concrete building with a red tile roof reminiscent of California architecture. St. Anthony's dance was only one of many going on at the same time. With its three large rooms, Wonderland had a heavy schedule of city functions and private celebrations—fund-raising dinners, awards ceremonies, and golden anniversary parties.

Another long-standing structure in Revere was directly across the street from the ballroom—Wonderland Dog Track, thirty acres of land dedicated to the sport of greyhound racing and the largest employer in the city. No matter how tight money was, my parents always had a little place in their budget for the activities at the dog track or Suffolk Downs Horse Track, the other recreational landmark in Revere. I remembered the evening of their seventeenth anniversary when they won fifty dollars by betting on seventeen in the daily double.

St. Anthony's dinner dances hadn't changed much in three decades. As we walked to our places in the ornate dining room, I saw the parish priests wearing their Roman collars going from table to table, mingling and schmoozing. Now and then one of the priests would beam at a proffered envelope, presumably contributions for the never-ending building fund drive. I could have sworn I saw many of the same people who'd been at The Fenway for pizza earlier in the week.

The music was designed for people like the four of us, who stopped learning new dances right before the twist. The orchestra played "things you can hum later," as Frank said. I began to suspect a conspiracy among my three friends to keep the conversation far from both hydrogen and murder. The closest we came to hitting on science was Peter's flattering remark.

"Gloria gave a wonderful talk on Enrico Fermi," he said.

"Tell us all about it," Frank said, rolling his eyes toward, the ceiling and we all laughed.

Strangely, the highlight of my evening came during a trip to the women's room with Rose. As we stood before the mirrored wall in the vestibule of the lounge, Rose stopped in the middle of applying lipstick to her already perfect makeup suite.

"I almost forgot to tell you two things," she said, using the long jeweled tube of Shades of Blue to emphasize her points. "See, I'm getting like you, Gloria, making mental lists."

"It comes in handy, doesn't it?"

"Well, I guess. So, here are the two things. First, Janice Bensen came to my office after the funeral this morning. She wanted me to identify who sent one of the larger baskets of flowers. The card was from Petrillo's Flower Shop and it just said, *Cherished Friend.* I don't know if that's interesting or not.''

''Very interesting,'' I said. ''What did you tell her?''

Having finished a meager repair job on my hair, I turned and sat on the counter, my back to the mirror, to face Rose while she was talking. We'd both checked out the population of the lounge and although no one was close enough to hear, we kept our voices to a near whisper. It was unusual for Rose to reveal anything about the conduct of her clients, living or dead, and I knew she didn't violate that policy easily.

''You know I won't say anything about this,'' I said, to reassure her.

''I know that, Gloria. I'm comfortable telling you this. I think of you as the police now.''

''Thanks, I think. So what did you tell her?''

''Just that I didn't know. The flowers and cards come in and Martha accepts them at the door usually. I told Janice she'd have to call the florist.''

''So you can't tell even if they were sent by someone out of state, for example?''

''No, only Jeannie at Petrillo's would know how the order came in.''

''Did Janice seem satisfied with your answer? Do you think she called Petrillo's?''

''My guess is yes. She was pretty upset. I think she thought I was holding out on her.''

''Would the florist tell her, or is that considered confidential?''

''It depends. Probably not if she went in there raving. But if she presented herself as a grieving widow who wanted to send thank-you notes to her late husband's friends, they might.''

''Would they tell anyone else?''

''They told me,'' Rose said, turning to me with a wide, smug smile.

"You mean you already checked? Why didn't you tell me?" My excitement was all the reward Rose needed, and the smile never left her face as she told me how she and Jeannie did a lot of business together.

"The flowers were ordered by an A. Lee from Berkeley, California."

I gave Rose a smile and sideways tilt of my head that to us always meant "thank you so much and I owe you."

"Next?" I asked, settling farther back on the cold marble countertop.

"Next what?"

Rose had continued to work on her face while she talked. I marveled at the equipment she could stuff into a tiny evening bag. Her blue sequined purse, not more than six inches across, held a set of creams, powders, and tools that would put an undergraduate physics supply room to shame.

"You said you had two things to tell me."

"Oh, right. See how the number thing doesn't work for me?" she said. I winced as she moved a sinister-looking pair of curved tongs towards her eyes. "The second thing is that Jim, the tall young guy who was saying the rosary at the wake? He was in with Eric's body really late last night."

"You mean after he left my apartment?"

Rose nodded.

"Sal, Robert's number-one man, was doing some work in the prep room. He came back through the foyer to get his jacket and saw a man kneeling in front of the casket. It was around midnight and Sal was a little nervous but he said the guy looked harmless so he went up to him and told him it was time to lock up. They walked out together and that was that. It's probably nothing, but I decided to tell you any little thing that's different."

"You did really well for someone who doesn't like to count," I said.

Rose beamed, showing me at once her pride of accomplishment and her new face.

* * *

Back at our table, Rose covered for me, helping me keep on track with the small talk, knowing that my mind was processing the two pieces of information she'd given me.

My mind was drifting for more reasons than Rose's detective work. Through the evening my feelings oscillated between comfort and familiarity with my old friends, and excitement at the prospect of a new friend and new experiences. As the four of us talked about the winter opera season and how we'd need to get tickets soon for the Messiah concerts by the Handel-Hayden Society of Boston, it was Matt's face I saw, not Peter's, in my mental vision.

I felt like a hypocrite enjoying ravioli and roast chicken that Peter had paid for while plotting how to tell him that this was probably our last date. Hard as it was, for a while I forgot about the long-term future and allowed myself to get caught up in the festive atmosphere of Wonderland, doing my share of dancing, eating, and humming.

When Peter and I arrived at Galigani's Mortuary after dropping Rose and Frank off at their home, I couldn't talk him out of walking me upstairs. It turned out to be a great blessing that he did.

My door stood slightly open, shreds of wood hanging around the brass lock plate, and my apartment had been trashed.

Chapter Eighteen

I looked at my overturned rocker and my books and papers strewn about and studied the scene as if I were examining a photograph at a museum exhibit. From the doorway I could see my three sofa cushions on the floor, forming a line to the kitchen, looking like a stepping-stone pathway to the stove.

I started to enter my living room, but Peter pulled me back and ushered me down the stairs to his car. We drove two blocks to a pay phone and called the police. Peter hadn't even let me run over to my coffee table to get my cordless phone.

I was in a daze as I followed his instructions, finally realizing that he was acting out of sensible caution—we couldn't be sure the burglar had left the apartment. I'd never been burgled before and I didn't know the protocol.

Twenty minutes later Peter and I sat in my kitchen with long faces, as if we were mourning a mutual friend. A uniformed policeman spread fine black powder over every flat surface in my apartment and a few curved ones. Peter had called Rose and Frank and made a pot of coffee. I'd done my best to answer the questions of a second officer. It disturbed me that I couldn't remember whether I'd set the alarm before we left for the dance. Peter was almost sure I hadn't.

"Did you have any cash around?" the officer asked.

"No, I don't usually keep any, outside of what's in my wallet."

"Have you seen anyone strange hanging around lately? Someone who shouldn't be here?"

"This is a funeral home," Peter said, in an aggravated tone.

He apologized to the officer so quickly that it came out almost as one sentence.

"I'm sorry," he said. "She shouldn't be living here in the first place. You're just doing your job."

Although I was too distraught to respond to his comment, I was alert enough to register it as one more reason the Gloria-and-Peter team would be history very soon.

"Can you tell us if anything's missing?" the officer asked. I guessed he'd seen enough domestic squabbling over the years to know he should ignore it.

"Nothing big," I said, glancing at my entertainment center, as the home decorating catalog called it. My television set, VCR, and CD player were still there, in an upright position. My computer station, wedged into a corner between the living room and kitchen, was also undisturbed, except that my file drawers had been rifled through.

"I'll have to take a closer look," I said, walking toward my bedroom.

I stepped around dresser drawers that had been pulled out to the end of their track or tipped onto the floor, struggling to ignore the knot in my stomach. My mirrored closet door was open; my shoe boxes had been emptied and transparent storage bags with sweaters and blankets were in a heap. Dresses and shirts still on hangers had been draped over the handles of my exercise bicycle as if they were part of a window display in progress. Compared to this scene, moving-in day was neat and orderly.

Without counting my separated pieces of clothing, I estimated that it was all there. In spite of the tight feeling all through my body, I smiled when I looked in the drawer of my night table, which had also been pulled open, and saw Al's little black book in plain sight next to a bag of cough drops. *At least I know it's not a Mafia hit,* I thought.

I checked my jewelry inventory. My pins, which were arranged in partitioned boxes I'd bought in a hardware store, appeared untouched in the top drawer of my dresser. My watches and necklaces, all inexpensive, were as I'd left them, in a half-dozen small china and wooden containers spread out across my dresser. None of the boxes was opened.

I glanced in my bathroom and sighed when I saw that all my towels had been swept from the closet shelves to the tile floor, some landing in the tub and toilet.

As I returned to the living room, I heard one of the officers deny Peter's request to let him start straightening up.

''Sgt. Gennaro wants to see it as is,'' the officer said.

Seconds later, Matt came through the door, red-faced and out of breath, looking like an overweight fifty-five-year-old who'd just run up two flights of stairs. He was wearing casual blue slacks, a white shirt, and a navy-blue crewneck sweater. He gave me a brief nod as his eyes swept across the living room and kitchen, floor to ceiling.

''Has anyone checked the attic?'' he asked.

The officers looked at each other and shrugged their shoulders. Their looks of surprise were matched by Peter's as Matt headed for the hallway behind my bedroom. I didn't look forward to explaining later to Peter just how come Matt was so familiar with the layout of my apartment.

I watched as Matt dragged the ladder to the trapdoor and once again disappeared into Galigani's attic while I waited below. He came back as dusty as he had the first time, and I had the silly thought of sweeping up there so it would be clean for him on his next trip.

''I'd like you to take a look up there,'' Matt said to me. ''See if you think anyone's been up there tonight.'' He looked at me, in my heels and pearls, still unaccountably clutching my small black satin evening bag, its long gold chain wrapped around my wrists. ''You might want to change first,'' he added.

Without speaking, I closed my bedroom door and leaned against it, close to tears. I imagined each piece of my clothing, my underwear and my sweaters, being touched by a stranger. My home had been entered, my privacy violated. I wanted at least to wash everything in hot water and soap, or preferably, throw every stitch away and start again. To make matters worse, Matt was clearly as unhappy as if this had been my fault.

More than tears, I fought against Josephine's philosophy that when bad things happen, it's because the universe hates you and there's no use trying to have a happy life. Most days I arrived home from school to find Josephine in a state of high stress over some incident, cursing the entire Holy Family—*Gesu, Giusseppe, Sant'Anna, e Maria.* If you didn't know her, you'd think some great tragedy had befallen her, but the cause of her raving could be as simple as a chickadee that had done its duty on the clean towels drying on her clothesline. Not a great way to train a child how to accept life's ups and downs.

I heard voices from the living room—Rose and Frank had arrived. I cleared my head and forced myself to change into jeans and a sweater, picking them out of an already opened drawer. I chose a set that I thought might not have been touched since they were at the bottom of a stack.

I climbed up to the attic and found nothing changed from Thursday evening. I sat back against the wall and hugged my knees to my chest. Looking out the small window at the clear night sky, I wanted to stay up there forever.

"Gloria?"

I heard Matt's voice and the creaking of the ladder under his weight. I got to my feet before he could see me in my fetal position.

"I don't think he was up here," I said, and started down the ladder, my knees wobbling, my eyes burning. By the time I reached bottom, I was breathing as normally as I could. Matt held my bedroom door open and looked at my face with an intensity I hadn't seen before.

"I'm fine," I said, in response to his gaze.

When I got back to the living room Rose put her arms around me. She'd changed into what she called her California look—the pink-and-turquoise sweat suit that she'd bought in a suburban mall during one of her visits to me. Her hair was still as perfectly coiffed as it had been at the dinner dance.

"I'm so glad you weren't here, Gloria," she said, holding on to me. Frank came over and rubbed my back.

"I don't think I set the alarm," I said. "I'm so sorry."

The alarm system was there to protect their business, and I felt I'd let my friends down.

I heard Matt ask Frank questions. Had the mortuary ever been broken into? Not in twenty years or more, when some flowers had been stolen and replaced with plastic ones as a prank. Who knew the code for the alarm system? The Galiganis and me, of course, and Rose's assistant, Martha. Was there anything valuable in the offices or the parlors? Rose's mother's furniture, but that was hardly what they were after unless they'd brought a large van.

"I'm going down through the other rooms with the officers," Frank said. "I tried the doors as we came up and they're all locked, so we probably won't find anything wrong."

When Matt turned to me and asked what time I'd left the apartment it dawned on me that he wouldn't know Peter. I included an awkward introduction as I gave Matt the timeline for the evening.

It was almost one-thirty in the morning before Matt sent the officers away. Peter and Rose had put the chairs upright and arranged all my leftovers on a tray—cheese, olives, pickles, crackers, chocolates, and cannoli. I finally stopped walking in circles and the five of us sat around my kitchen table with coffee and a makeshift antipasto.

"Do you have any idea what someone might have been looking for?" Matt asked me.

"No," I said, surprised at the question. I'd assumed that a random thief had entered the unalarmed house to look around for cash or small items he could fence.

"You think Gloria's apartment was targeted?" Peter asked. He was still wearing his tie, but didn't look quite as neat and pressed as he had earlier in the evening. His voice, sounding tired and worried, showed the stress of the last hour and a half.

"What we have," Matt said, "is someone comes in, skips the other two floors even though those locks are easier to crack, and heads up here. Then he tosses the place but doesn't take anything."

"Maybe he saw there was nothing valuable. I have only costume jewelry and no cash."

"Everything has value in a random burglary. These guys are scavengers. Someone comes all this way, he's going to take the jewelry, the computer keyboard, the CDs, something to make the trip worth it," Matt said.

"It has to do with Gloria's work on the Bensen murder case, doesn't it?" Peter said.

"Maybe she shouldn't be doing this," Rose said.

I heard myself being talked about as if I were asleep in the next room. I felt that I should be participating, but I couldn't get any words out.

Matt turned to me. The bags under his eyes were deeper than I'd ever seen them, but he was clean-shaven. I wondered if he shaved before going to bed every night in case he got a midnight summons. I wondered if I'd ever know.

"I know it's tough to think about this now. But let's give it one more try. Are you fairly sure nothing's missing? A rare book? A collection of some kind? Stamps or coins?"

"I don't have anything like that."

"Legal papers? Documents that might be important to someone else?"

"Nothing."

I put my head down, stared at the gray carpet tufts, and tried to conjure up an inventory of everything I had in the apartment. The most expensive thing I owned was my computer system and that hadn't been touched. I look around the room, and as my eyes came back into focus, I noticed something on my writing desk that hadn't been there earlier.

"My briefcase," I said, pointing across the room.

"I found that in Rose's office when I was there a few minutes ago with the officers," Frank said. "I knew it was yours so I brought it up."

"Someone was looking for my briefcase."

"Is there something valuable in it?" Rose asked.

Chapter Nineteen

While Matt went over to get my briefcase I gave the others a two-line summary of where the computer printout came from and how Connie had confessed to tampering with the gas gun data.

"Then why would anyone want to steal the printout, if the fraud is already out in the open?" Peter asked.

"Maybe they don't all know it's out in the open," Frank said.

"They all know," Matt said. "At least all the principals. We took care of that today."

Matt was pacing up and down my living room, scratching his head. When his back was to me, I could see the bulge of his gun stuck in his belt under his sweater. I preferred the holster-hidden-by-a-jacket look myself. I wondered if he had a switchblade hidden in his sock, or if only vice cops did that.

I turned back to the printout.

"It must be these three symbols," I said. "I've always thought they meant something." I pointed to the bottom of the last page. "I'll just have work harder at figuring out what."

As if insects were flying around them, my guests shook their heads and uttered different forms of "no, you don't." I'd expected it from Peter or Rose, but I was surprised that Frank was also in agreement.

I ignored them all and looked at Matt, who for all practical purposes was my boss in these matters. He looked at his watch.

''We shouldn't make any decisions at this hour,'' he said. ''It's time to think about where you're going to stay for the rest of the night.''

''Right here,'' I said, my arm sweeping across my apartment to point to my bedroom, as if I were a game show hostess.

Once I could make sense out of the burglary I was less fearful. I reasoned that the state of my apartment fit the pattern of a person looking for a large stack of papers or a briefcase. He didn't open small jewelry boxes or disturb obvious areas like my TV or computer center. He probably thought I could have removed the printout from the briefcase and hidden it, so he'd looked in files and drawers and underneath cushions. It all made sense, so I was no longer afraid.

''Now that he thinks I don't have the printout,'' I said, ''he won't come back.''

I tried to sound logical and confident, which worked as long as I didn't dwell on the thought that this abstract burglar was most likely also Eric's murderer.

''He doesn't know where you were,'' Peter said. ''Maybe he thinks you had it with you. He didn't find it, so of course he'll be back.'' Once again, Peter's logic and mine clashed.

''Come home with us, Gloria,'' Rose said. ''Just for tonight.''

Matt had walked over to the door to my apartment, then to my phone. He caught my eye and we exchanged looks and nods that said yes, he could use it.

I tuned out Peter and Rose and Frank who were talking about me again.

''She's crazy to want to stay on this case,'' Peter said.

''She's a big girl, Peter,'' Rose said, reminding me why she should get a lifetime achievement award for friendship.

Matt returned from his phone calls with what sounded like a nonnegotiable decision.

''Our guy's coming over to fix the door and put in a new lock,'' he said. ''And an unmarked police car will be out front until further notice. I'll wait here until it's all set up. You can all go home and get some sleep.''

Rose frowned a bit, but didn't comment, and Frank seemed satisfied.

''It's like getting back up on the horse,'' he said. ''A person shouldn't give in.''

Frank wasn't any better at figures of speech than Rose was, but I was grateful for his support.

Peter was clearly the least happy with the arrangement.

''I'm not through with this,'' he said as he left, using the possessive tone that I'd fought against a few days before. This time I was too tired for a smart-aleck comeback and gave him a patronizing smile instead. It never occurred to me to thank him for the evening of dinner and dancing and for being so supportive in an emergency situation.

With my friends gone, I tried to process the fact that I was sitting in my apartment at two in the morning with Sgt. Matt Gennaro, at the end of an evening that began with a date with Peter Mastrone.

We'd both switched to decaf coffee and sat opposite each other in my living room. Matt was on the couch leaning over the coffee table writing in his notebook. I studied the bald spot at the back of his head and wondered if he knew it was there. I remembered my father's surprise at seeing his in a department store monitor as he stood under a surveillance camera.

''Are you going to fire me?'' I asked.

He laughed and rubbed his hand across his chin. He gave me a look I would have called intimate in other circumstances. Since he first came in I'd wanted to fix his shirt collar, half of which was under the crewneck of his sweater and half over it. My old-school conservatism came to my rescue before I made a fool of myself. *I may preach raving feminism,* I thought, *but I'm still going to wait for him to make the first move.*

''Not yet,'' Matt said.

It took a moment for me to connect his phrase to my question about being fired, not my unspoken thoughts about romantic moves.

"At this point, I think you're right about the doodles at the end of the printout," he said, pulling at the tufts of gray hair around his ear. "I can't imagine why else you'd have had this break-in. I'd like you to keep thinking about the printout, but we'll have to find a way to make it absolutely safe for you. I have a plan that I think will work."

The phone rang and we both jumped a bit. The ring had the unique sound that phones always seem to have after midnight, even if you're up and dressed. I answered and heard Peter's voice.

"Are you okay?" he asked. "Is the cop still there?"

"Yes and yes."

"Well, I just wanted to make sure. I think you should have gone home with Rose and Frank."

I sighed loudly enough, I hoped, for Peter to hear a message of exasperation.

"Thanks for checking. I'll call you tomorrow."

"Call me tomorrow," he said, as if it were his idea.

I still hadn't thanked him for the evening and although I thought of doing it, I didn't want to have that conversation in Matt's presence. Matt had walked over to the far wall of my living room and was looking at my books, photographs, and memorabilia scattered around on the shelves. I appreciated what seemed to be a gesture toward giving me privacy without a lot of options in my small apartment. When I hung up with Peter, Matt returned to the sofa.

"Your boyfriend?" he asked.

So much for privacy, but I was glad to have a chance to explain Peter.

"Peter's an old friend," I said, emphasizing the difference. "He wanted to make sure everything was still all right. We went to the St. Anthony's dance at Wonderland tonight with Rose and Frank. I've known them all since fourth grade at the old Lincoln School. Except I didn't really have contact with Peter these last thirty years. I just met him again when I came back to Revere. Actually, just this week.''

I stopped, looked up at the ceiling and down again, acutely aware that I'd been rambling. *This must be how Matt gets confessions from murder suspects,* I thought. *Ask a casual two-word question and let the guy convict himself.*

''You probably didn't want to know all that,'' I said.

''As a matter of fact, I did.''

I swallowed and noticed stirrings in all the danger zones of my body.

''Is there anything else you'd like to know?'' I asked.

He sat back and crossed his legs, one arm along the back of the sofa.

''A lot.''

And there in my ransacked apartment, I felt a surge of happiness to rival any other joy in my life. I wished I could explain to Josephine how this was possible.

''Ask away,'' I said.

''Is your friend a scientist?''

''Which friend?'' I asked, laughing at the thought of Peter's being mistaken for a scientist, and at the same time determined to situate him as one among many friends on a long list.

''Peter.''

''Peter's about as anti-science and technology as you can get,'' I said. ''He doesn't have a microwave oven or a car phone and he thinks calculators mean the end of quality education as we know it.''

''Is he smart?''

As he asked this, Matt waved his arm in the direction of my bookcases. I wasn't sure what he meant and decided to take no chances.

''He teaches history and Italian at Revere High.''

''So he's smart, but not necessarily your caliber.''

''Do I have a caliber? Like a gun?''

That drew a laugh, a deep, warm laugh, and a slight shake of his head. *If this is flirting,* I thought, *I like it.*

''You know what I mean,'' he said. ''The guys at the station call you a brain. They're all afraid to talk to you.''

"Not George Berger," I said.

"Berger's okay, he's just young. He still has a lot to prove, and I think you intimidate him."

"Well, we're even," I said. "I'm intimidated by policemen."

"Because . . . ?"

"Because you carry weapons and have a lot of power and authority."

"To make up for no brains?"

"That's not what I meant," I said, afraid I was about to flunk flirting.

At that moment a tall young man in a khaki jumpsuit knocked on my half-open door. Poor timing.

"Joey," Matt said, and waved him in.

Matt introduced me to Joey, a police department lock expert who looked young enough to be my grandson. While Joey worked on my door with a strange-looking tool he'd taken from his wide leather belt, Matt and I resumed the business talk we'd strayed from. Matt explained his plan—he'd call the principals together for a meeting as soon as possible, preferably Sunday afternoon. We noted that it might be difficult to arrange since it was already well into Sunday morning.

Matt would tell everyone who'd been questioned in the case that my work was over, that he was pursuing other lines of inquiry. Meanwhile, I was to keep working on the printout.

"Can you just write down that last line of characters for your use and give me the printout with all your red notes? That way they'll figure you don't have a copy."

"That's fine," I said. "Whatever this line of type is, I don't think it's connected to the rest of the data. And, believe me, I know the characters by heart."

"You think Eric was trying to tell us who his killer was, like in the movies?" Matt asked.

"I guess I do. He might have had a split-second to hit three keys that would identify the person. Is it only amateurs who come up with things like that?''

''No. It happens.''

''But you don't think so in this case?''

''I try to keep an open mind.''

I wasn't satisfied, but I knew that was all I was going to get.

Joey signaled that he was finished. He closed and opened the door for me twice.

''It's better than it was before your break-in,'' he said, and showed me a new pin that made it harder to jimmy the lock.

I thanked him and offered him coffee or a soft drink, but he said he had another stop to make across town. Joey reassembled his belt and said good night. I wondered if the department kept locksmiths on duty all night. There was a lot I didn't know about the police business, I realized, watching Matt and Joey exchange forms and signatures.

Matt walked over to my window and looked down at the street. When I imagined that he saw a lamppost and a man in an overcoat smoking a cigarette in the shadows, I knew the strain of the evening had caught up with me.

''The unmarked is there,'' Matt said, bringing me out of the realm of Bogart movies. ''I hope you can get some sleep.''

''I hope you can, too. Do you want me at that meeting this afternoon?''

''I'll let you know, but right now I don't think so. It's probably better if they don't see us together.''

''You mean we have to stop meeting this way?'' I asked, before I could stop myself.

Matt had stuffed his notebook and pencil into his pants pocket and was at the door. He turned and gave me a broad smile.

''Until after the case,'' he said, and left.

I locked the door behind him and went over to the couch. I sat in the spot he'd been in during our most personal conversation to date. *Next time this happens,* I told myself, *I'm going to fix his collar.*

Chapter Twenty

Without a glance at the shower or my toothbrush, I took off my jeans and sweater, wrapped myself in a robe, and got into bed. I slept really well for someone who had to climb over ravaged drawers of clothing and an upside-down lamp on the floor to get to her pillow. I looked at the black fingerprint powder on my night table and thought of Josephine, who couldn't sleep if there was so much as a dirty coffee cup in the sink or an open newspaper on a chair. I asked her forgiveness under these special circumstances.

Throughout the morning I heard the bells from St. Anthony's tower announcing the hourly Sunday masses, but they became part of my dreams, which were strangely peaceful. The only recognizable figure was my father dressed in his paint-splattered overalls showing me his bald spot and telling me to take care of myself.

It was almost noon before I was fully awake. I wandered around my apartment, picking up towels and shoes, like a bag lady after a storm. I created a large pile of clothing and linens, mentally labeled it "laundry" and rewarded myself with the last cannoli. The two-day-old pastry shell was soggy and the cream had the consistency of rubber cement, but I ate it anyway. I had the crazy thought that I'd better stock my refrigerator in case I ended up with a house full of company for the third night in a row.

I considered calling Matt to ask about the meeting, or Peter to apologize for my abruptness on the phone. I decided to go easy on myself and started with Rose.

"What a night," she said. "I didn't know what time you'd get to bed, so I didn't want to call too early."

"You mean you didn't know if I'd be alone."

She laughed and I heard a distinctly hopeful sound from her throat. I hated to let her down.

"I slept alone," I said. "But there was a—uh—a little hint of something." *How articulate,* I thought, but my stuttering was enough to make Rose gasp.

"We have to talk," she said, and we agreed to meet for a late lunch at Kelly's Roast Beef, at the north end of Revere Beach.

I left a message on Matt's voice mail at his office to tell him I was available for a meeting. I gave him the number for my cellular phone and dressed for my first walk on the beach. My red windbreaker hanging in my hall closet was the right weight and showed no signs of being handled by strangers the night before. I shoved the phone into the long front pocket across my waist and headed out.

With a gusty wind lifting sand into the fifty-degree air, few people were out of their cars along Revere Beach Boulevard. Traffic flowed beside me at a steady pace towards the Point of Pines. *They're probably all going to Kelly's,* I thought, remembering the long lines waiting there for roast beef sandwiches and clam plates all year round.

I walked about a half mile in the opposite direction from Kelly's, most of it through the sand, dark and muddy down near the waterline, light and soft near the cement boardwalk. The ocean was on my left, curving in front of me as I headed south along the beach. I took my rhythm from the pounding surf, giving myself up to its power, as if I could take in some of its energy and make it my own, as if with the ocean at my side I could be anything I wanted to be. *For all we know about hydrogen,* I thought, *we don't know enough about the ocean.*

I crossed the street where the old red brick bathhouse used to be. The bright blue sign on a tall post outside the building identified it now as the home of the State Police. Enormous apartment buildings with tiny balconies stood a few yards to the north, which I estimated to be the former site of the Cyclone, the old roller coaster.

I pictured myself on that spot at fourteen years old. Dressed in a starched white cotton blouse, I'd made pink cotton candy for fifty cents an hour while sleek metal cars whirled and screeched above me, like unruly children playing tag on thirty-six-hundred feet of track. I was glad I was three thousand miles away in 1974 when a wrecking crew tore down the charred remains of what was once called the fastest ride in the world. Since returning to my childhood home, I found I could dwell on the past for a long time. I wanted to ask Rose if it was any different for her, since she had lived her whole life on the same streets.

Rose was fourth in line by the time I retraced my steps and walked north to Kelly's. Her short frame was dwarfed by the people around her lined up at the counter. In her most grubby look, designer jeans and hooded sweatshirt, Rose looked better than most people on their way to a wedding.

"Good timing," she said. "What are you drinking?"

"Water. A lot of it," I said, licking my lips at the thought of a tall bottle of spring water and a lobster roll. I'd walked fast enough to keep warm and to feel deserving of a feast.

We took our food across the street. Passing up the cold, wet benches of the pavilion, populated by swarms of pigeons and sea gulls, we ate in Rose's station wagon. Families on both sides of us had the same idea, turning their minivans into picnic areas. Rose had parked facing the ocean and for a while we watched the gray-green waves and ate in silence, with the sound of the surf as background.

"I'm ready to hear about the hint," Rose said when we'd finished our sandwiches. "The Matt Gennaro hint of . . . what was it? But only if you want to tell me."

I did want to tell her, my forever friend, what I was feeling. If I were going to make a fool of myself in front of anyone, I wanted it to be Rose. I told her about Matt's parting comment, and asked her what she thought I should do about Peter.

I felt like a fourteen-year-old on her break from making cotton candy.

"I'm not sure whether anything is possible with Matt," I told her. "But after last night I'm sure of two things."

"Let's have your list," Rose said, in her usual way of making fun of my constant need for mentally organizing and counting everything.

"One, I'd like to see Matt socially, and two, I'll never feel anything for Peter beyond friendship."

"Clear enough. You have no obligation to Peter," she said, picking at the straw in her large iced tea. "But I think you need to be more direct with him."

"Instead of sarcastic?"

"Well, I know sarcasm is more fun, but you're not getting through to Peter. You know how hard he's trying when he starts including science in his lesson plans."

"You're right. And since there's nothing I can do about the Matt thing until this investigation is over, I should be working to help solve the case as quickly as possible."

Rose drove us to the mortuary and made a pretense of having to make a stop at her office.

"I'm not afraid to go up alone," I said.

"I am," she said. "I'll feel better seeing you arrive home with no surprises today."

Rose came upstairs with me and stayed around for a while, straightening the area around my bed. Without a doubt it was less depressing to have help and companionship clearing up the mess.

As we worked, I pictured the chief Bensen murder suspects in my apartment, one at a time. Leder picking through my nightgowns and pantyhose with lecherous fingers. Connie in her career-minded business suit methodically searching the files next to my computer. Janice in a silk pants suit looking through my clothes, disgusted with the contents of my wardrobe. Jim making the sign of the cross as he tipped over my glide rocker. Andrea checking to see if I had any superheroes among my knickknacks while she rifled through my desk.

None of the images rang true, but I didn't want to return to the random-victim theory of my burglary either.

As soon as Rose left, I put on a CD of the Three Tenors and went back to my original case notes, with its star system of guilt. I'd given Leder four stars as my first choice, and his phone call to me supported my thinking. But Janice, who wasn't even on my original list, was acting the strangest. Why would she care who sent flowers to her dead husband unless she were unbalanced in some way? When it came right down to it, I still envisioned murderers as unbalanced. I wished I knew more about the psychology of killers and wondered how soon I'd be able to ask Matt to teach me about homicidal maniacs.

Most of Jim's behavior for the last week was normal for Jim. Taking care of everyone's needs, praying the rosary in public. But his late-night appearance at the prie-dieu in front of Eric's body seemed to me overdoing it. If it weren't for his outburst on the way to funeral, I would have chalked it up to genuine concern for the salvation of Eric's soul. But after seeing the intensity of his anger at what he perceived as immoral behavior on Eric's part, I wondered if his religious zeal could lead him to murder.

I reviewed my notes on Connie and Andrea and couldn't come up with anything new. Their behavior was at opposite ends of the emotional spectrum, telling me nothing about their guilt or innocence. The fact that the other "other woman," Annie, had sent flowers didn't amount to any solid information either.

Once again I had no idea whether to tell all this to Matt. Andrea's eavesdropping on Leder's phone conversation with his wife. Jim's extra prayers and self-righteous evangelism. Annie's flowers. Were these bits of meaningless gossip or important clues in an investigation? I was beginning to feel like a den mother trying to keep track of the movements of all her little Brownies.

Worse than that, I realized that my decisions about how to handle the information were governed by my fear of Matt's disapproval. I couldn't bear his thinking of me as either an inept investigator or a meddling civilian who trafficked in rumors. It was a bad sign, I told myself, when I was attracted to a man who inspired the same feelings in me that Josephine had.

After a while, I put the people side of the case away and found my notes on the elusive printout characters, Δμ∫. I'd drawn lines to make three columns on a piece of paper and put each character at the top of a column. Under each character I'd written out all the common physical meanings for it in standard textbooks. I even included the muon, an elementary particle represented by a μ, and found in cosmic radiation, although I couldn't think of the slightest reason for the muon to be involved in Eric's hydrogen research.

Separately the characters had little significance to the computer program, and together they had even less. I decided to leave that exercise for a while and had just booted up my computer to balance my checkbook and pay some bills, when the phone rang. The conversation I'd been putting off all day.

"I saw your so-called unmarked police guard outside the building on my way to mass this morning," Peter said. "If I could tell it was a cop car, I'm sure a burglar could tell."

In the last couple of days I'd been irritated with Peter's use of the word "cop," spitting it out in his references to Matt especially. It seemed a deliberate deviation from his usual formal, elegant speech patterns.

"Maybe that's the idea," I said. "Scare away the bad guys."

"Gloria, you're being very difficult."

No sarcasm, I remembered, and softened my voice.

"You're right, Peter. And in all the excitement, I never thanked you for the evening. The tea roses still look good. I have them in a mug on my table."

"Excitement is not the word I'd use. Danger is more like it."

I held the phone receiver away from my ear and looked at it, as if to ask what it wanted of me.

"Well, it's over," I said, "and I'm sorry you had to be part of it."

"I'd really like to have a talk, Gloria. I haven't seen you alone for more than ten minutes."

"We can have a talk now," I said, departing from my usual tendency to keep phone conversations brief. I've always needed visual input to fully understand what's being said to me. I liked to use the phone to set up meetings, not to hold meetings.

"I'd like to see you," he said. "Just the two of us, for a conversation."

Peter sounded frustrated and I wrestled with how cooperative I should be. Besides that, I didn't know for sure if Rose was right. If Peter had no romantic intentions, I certainly didn't want to put ideas into his head. *Maybe he's going to tell me he just wants to be friends,* I thought. I decided he deserved one more face-to-face encounter.

"I'm free this evening," I said.

"I'll pick up something and see you at six."

I knew that when Peter picked up something, it would be better than anything I could have prepared, even if I spent all day cooking. My guess was that he'd make a quick trip to Boston's North End and carry out gourmet pesto sauce.

On my second attempt to work at my computer, I heard a soft knock. I stopped in my tracks a few feet from the door and felt a brief, unfamiliar shiver of fear. *It's the middle of a sunny afternoon and I'm in my own living room,* I told myself. *Let's not overreact. Let's also ask Frank to have a peephole installed,* I added.

Another knock, and then, "It's Matt Gennaro."

Until I saw his face, I thought nothing could have made the

day sunnier than a visit from Matt. He was in his business blues again and his shoulders sagged as if they were bearing the weight of the bad news he'd come to give me.

"Ralph Leder's been murdered," he said.

Chapter Twenty-one

I sat down on my rocker without offering Matt a drink, or a chair for that matter. He came over to me and put his hand on my shoulder, but I hardly felt it. I was facing my bookcases, which seemed to be toppling over, spilling books and photographs onto my carpet. I blinked several times until they came into focus back in their rightful places, like an exercise in reverse entropy.

"I wanted to tell you before it hits the news," Matt said, waving his arm in the direction of my television set.

Leder had remained high on my list as the one most likely to be Eric's murderer, especially once Connie confessed to the cover-up. In my mind, it added up. He'd masterminded the data fraud and murdered Eric when he threatened to expose it. Hadn't he called to warn me not to pursue that line of investigation? He also owned a gun and his alibi was weak since his wife could have been knocked out with sleeping pills the night of Eric's murder. Not only that, he was sexist, and I didn't like him.

I wouldn't have been surprised to read about Leder's arrest in the Boston newspapers, but hearing about his murder threw me off balance. The voice of Luciano Pavarotti bounced around in my living room and in my brain, the last aria on the disk, *Vincero*—I shall win.

"Are you all right?"

Matt had been standing over me while I sat with my hand pressed against my forehead. As he handed me a glass of water, apparently from my kitchen, I wondered how long I'd been lost in my thoughts.

"I'm sorry," I said. "Thank you for telling me this way."

Not one to be outdone in service in my own apartment, I made coffee. But I was almost completely out of solid food except for three chocolates, and felt embarrassed as I told this to Matt. He patted his narrow leather belt and said he'd had a late lunch.

Matt took a seat on the couch. He leaned over the coffee table in front of him, put down his mug, and picked up my notes on the printout characters. He rolled the page into a long tube and tapped his leg with it.

"I'm not sure what we're dealing with here. It could be a psycho out for every physicist in Suffolk County, for all we know. I'd like you to forget about this case."

"I'm really over the shock," I said. "Was Leder's the same kind of murder as Eric's?"

"Leder was shot, apparently with the same gun, but I haven't had the final word on that."

"Did you have your meeting?"

"No, this new development got in the way. I postponed it till tomorrow morning. But I don't want you there. You're off the case."

"I think I'm close to figuring out the code," I said, hoping my lying nose wasn't stretched out past the coffee table. "How about one more day? Let me come to the meeting in the morning and give me until six o'clock tomorrow evening."

Matt stood up and shook his head. He held my notes in both hands, as if he were ready to tear them to shreds. "I guess I'm not being clear," he said. "You're off the case."

I tried to recall every assertiveness tip I'd ever read about and made a pronouncement that may have startled Matt. It certainly startled me.

"You can't just pull me off," I said. "I have a contract."

The CD had ended, and my voice boomed out into the silence. He sat down again, leading me to believe I'd scored a victory. *Maybe there's something to this 1990s self-confidence,* I thought.

His voice was soft and had none of the scolding tone I remembered from the stormy visit he'd paid me after I'd entertained murder suspects. *Double* murder suspects, I reminded myself.

"I'm worried about you," he said. "I don't want anything to happen to you."

"I appreciate that. But I'm not going to sue the department or anything."

Matt took a deep breath. I felt my stomach turn over as he looked directly at me, his eyes close to pleading.

"Do you really think that's what I'm worried about?" he said.

I thought my heart was banging out loud, until I realized it was a knock at my door. I looked at my watch. Six o'clock.

Peter was at my door, and Matt was on my couch, and except for the two murders hanging in the air, I felt like the centerpiece of a French comedy.

"Come in, Peter, you know Sgt. Matt Gennaro."

I took a brown paper grocery sack from Peter's hand and carried it to the kitchen, thus avoiding his gaze. He walked over and shook Matt's hand.

"Matt has terrible news," I said. "Dr. Leder, who was Eric Bensen's mentor, was found murdered also."

"I hope this is the end of it, Gloria," Peter said, shaking his head. "This is serious business. It's a job for the police, not for amateurs."

"Two people I know have been murdered," I said, grateful at least that Peter hadn't said "cop." "If there's a way I can help find the person who did it, I can't just walk away."

As I said this, I turned my head back and forth, Ping-Pong style, between Peter and Matt. I hoped I sounded sure of myself.

"I was just leaving," Matt said. "I wanted to give Gloria the news in person."

I was distressed that he didn't respond to me and more upset that he thought he had to apologize to Peter for being there. I walked him to the door. I put my left hand on his and with my right hand slid the tube of notes up and out of his fist. I was close enough to catch his smell, a neutral shaving-cream odor rather than a scent from an aftershave.

"I'll see you in the morning," I said. "Did you say ten o'clock?"

"Nine," he said, his face in the scrunched-up configuration of a good loser as he left my apartment. I wanted to think I'd won him over by a combination of impeccable logic that appealed to his brain, and a sensuous touch that appealed to the rest of him.

Peter had gone to the kitchen and filled my spaghetti pot with water.

"I made a quick trip to the North End and picked up some pesto sauce," he said.

There's something to be said for predictability, I thought; *one of the linchpins of the scientific method.* Why not make it a requirement for a personal relationship? Matt brought me surprises—two personal searches of my home in the late-evening hours, a private security guard, two murders. Peter brought me what I expected from a suitor—chocolates, roses, and gourmet pesto sauce.

I watched Peter make himself at home in my kitchen, filling it with the smell of garlic and basil, and tried to imagine him in my future. With one of my aprons covering his forest-green polo shirt, he looked like an advertisement for Mother's Day cards.

"Your fridge is empty, Gloria," Peter said. "Do you get enough nutrition?"

At that, Peter's face went out of my future and Matt's came in. *What a way to make decisions,* I thought, but there it was. Both men seemed to be trying to take care of me—something I'd managed pretty well without for my entire adult life—but Matt's solicitude seemed more respectful, less possessive. Or maybe it was just chemistry, the non-laboratory kind. I pictured Matt in my bedroom emptying his pockets of handcuffs, loose change, and an index card with the Miranda rights typed on it.

Peter and I sat at my kitchen table and ate freshly made pasta, garlic bread, and tossed salad, all from Mangia's in the North End. I'd found some Girl Scout cookies in the freezer and created a respectable dessert by crumbling mint chocolate wafers over vanilla ice cream.

As we carried our coffee into the living room, I had the sense that our talk was about to begin. It was nice of him to wait until we'd finished dinner, I noted. During my childhood, mealtimes were always stressful, with unpleasant, critical conversations. Josephine used supper as a forum to bring up whatever was bothering her, usually about me, while my father sat eating his macaroni and meatballs, his head a few centimeters from his plate, no help at all.

Many years after my mother died, my father said to me, ''Your mother was very hard on you. I don't know why. She was just very hard on you.''

That was the only closure I was ever able to get about my unhappy childhood.

Peter cleared his throat.

''Gloria, I heard you tell the cop you'd see him tomorrow. Why are you being so stubborn?''

''Is this our talk?''

''You're making fun of me. I don't appreciate that.''

We were sitting on my glide rockers, across the coffee table from each other. The dinner music, a CD of Neapolitan folk songs, was still playing. Music from the old country for an old-fashioned conversation. I dug into my store of new-fashioned pop psychology phrases.

''I feel that you're trying to take over my life,'' I said. ''I'm not used to having people tell me what I can and can't do.''

''Maybe it's time to let someone take care of you.''

''That's not what I want, Peter.''

''You never answered my letters when I wrote that first year or two.''

"I thought I did."

"Well, you sent postcards of the redwoods and the Pacific Ocean, if that's what you mean."

"I had a lot to work through, Peter. And my graduate program was very demanding."

Peter was sitting with his legs crossed, his right ankle over his left knee. His voice sounded like that of the chairman of the board who has a certain number of agenda items to cover. From the white skin on the tips of his knuckles, I sensed that he thought he was losing some important vote.

"You never married. Did you ever come close?" he asked.

"Not even close," I said, coming up behind him from the kitchen. "How about you?"

I didn't like the way our little talk was going, but I decided to cooperate. To gain some distance from the touchy subjects, I refilled our coffee mugs and took the empty dessert dishes to the sink.

"Because of Al?" he asked, skipping right over my question about the history of his love life. I figured he could tell by my tone that I didn't really care about the answer.

"Because it just never came up," I said.

"What if I bring it up?"

"Let's not do this," I said. "We haven't seen each other in thirty years. Why don't we see if we can be friends first?"

I was proud of myself for coming up with a nice compromise, hoping Peter didn't interpret "friends" as people who go on cruises to the Caribbean together. I thought I was offering something open-ended, gentle but not misleading, the perfect win-win solution. Peter apparently thought less of my bottom line than I did.

"While you date one of Revere's finest?" he asked.

"I certainly hope so," I said.

Peter looked at his watch and stood up.

"I'd better be going," he said.

I guessed our talk was over.

* * *

After Peter left, I sat on my rocker for a long time wrapped in guilt because in spite of Rose's warning, I'd resorted to sarcasm again. *Maybe there's no good way to tell a person that his romantic interest in you is not mutual. Maybe right now Matt's having the same problem,* I thought, *deciding how to let me down gently.*

Having had enough emotion for one evening, I turned to the comfort of physics. I picked up *Scientific American* and treated my brain to an article on fusion energy research and helium, thinking life might be simpler one step higher than hydrogen in the periodic table.

For further enjoyment, and in keeping with the oscillator pattern of my mood, I turned to browsing the World Wide Web. I clicked on one of my favorite sites, pages of graphics from the Vatican Art Collection, and enjoyed the magnificent paintings of Michelangelo and Raphael in my own living room.

Once my computer was booted up, I made a gesture toward efficiency and decided to work on my laser project. I had only a few more sections to add and I'd have a complete lesson, ready for teachers to use with junior high students.

For the hands-on part of the lesson, I'd written an experiment using a water hose. Students would compare the sprays of water coming from the nozzle of the hose at different settings with the sprays of light coming from a regular flashlight and a laser. I wrote a few paragraphs of texts and equations to help the teacher explain the parallel—just as the narrower beam of water had more power than the wider beam, the narrower beam of light from the laser would have more power than the spread-out beam of a flashlight.

At midnight I went to bed with thoughts of seeing Matt the next day. But when I realized I'd have nothing more to tell him about the printout, the idea didn't seem so pleasant, especially if Berger were back by now.

I arrived at Matt's office a little before nine o'clock, wearing a three-piece knit suit that was identical to the striped one

I'd worn to Eric's wake, except that this one was in two shades of burgundy. Since it's not always easy to find attractive professional clothing in large sizes, I'd followed Josephine's advice, "If it fits, buy two." I pinned a small gold replica of San Francisco's Golden Gate Bridge, a gift from Elaine, to my jacket.

Matt was behind his desk in a brown suit and striped beige shirt, both of which looked new. His tie was as dark brown as his eyes, and the effect was of someone who'd just had his colors done. *Maybe Monday is dress-up day,* I thought.

"This is your swan song, right?" Matt said as I sat down.

It amused me that he was using participatory democracy, appearing to ask my permission. He'd apparently abandoned the benevolent despot role he'd assumed on three different occasions in my apartment. I was starting to feel like an expert in asserting myself with men. *And at such a young age,* I thought, not above a little self-inflicted sarcasm.

"Is that the best you can do for a greeting?" I asked.

"Didn't I ever tell you I'm crazy about swans?" he said.

Chapter Twenty-two

Connie and Jim came in right behind me, dissipating the effects of Matt's words on my complexion. If they hadn't both looked so distraught, I would have worried that I looked as though Matt and I had been caught in an embrace. But their grim faces brought me back to reality and I worried about them instead, wondering how they got the news of Leder's murder. Probably not as painlessly as I had, I guessed.

"Let's move to an interview room down the hall," Matt said. "I'll have someone direct Andrea and Janice when they get here."

"I can't believe this," Connie said to no one in particular, as we walked past desks and ringing phones. "First Eric, now Ralph."

Except for her casual use of Leder's first name, Connie seemed as uncomposed as I'd ever seen her, a tight ponytail pulling on the skin around her ears. She clutched her attaché case, holding it close to her chest as if it were a pile of schoolbooks without a handle.

"I brought my conductivity notes," she said to me, "just in case."

Soon after Jim had helped Matt arrange chairs around a gray metal table, Janice and Andrea were ushered into the room by a young policewoman. Andrea looked at me and shrugged her shoulders as if to give me a private sign that probably meant she was wrong about Leder, but I didn't pursue the interaction.

"Do you have any clues you can tell us about?" Janice asked Matt, taking a seat next to him.

Matt shook his head and straightened the small pile of papers he'd carried in.

''We're following some leads,'' he said. ''But first, coffee. I know it's early.''

Matt pointed to a side table and Jim acted as waiter for a few minutes, pouring coffee. I thought of asking him for a doughnut but I was afraid he'd take me seriously and run out to a bakery. More than that, a joke seemed out of place. This was the most solemn gathering of our group, surpassing even Eric's wake in gravity. Two murders seemed more than our little dinner group could handle.

We settled in our chairs and waited for Matt to speak, all eyes turned in his direction.

''I have a few things I want you all to hear,'' Matt said. ''Then I'll need a brief private session with each of you. I know you're all anxious to move on.''

Matt took a sip of his coffee and the five of us followed suit, as if we were playing Simon Says. As I glanced around the table, I couldn't decide which member of the group looked more shell-shocked.

Andrea, looming larger than ever in a shapeless denim jumper, seemed out of place, like a child admitted by mistake to a kindergarten faculty meeting. Janice picked at her Styrofoam cup in an uncharacteristically nervous gesture.

''The good news,'' Matt said, ''is that we're no longer pursuing technical issues in these cases, so you don't have to answer any more of Gloria's questions.''

If his intent was to lighten the mood, Matt succeeded at least in part. We all relaxed our bodies a little, smiled, and shifted in our chairs.

''You have another theory?'' Jim asked, sitting forward in his chair. Jim had chosen the least comfortable furniture in the room, a gray folding chair with a hard metal seat.

''We're off the hook,'' Connie said, extending the new, lighter atmosphere and placing her attaché case down on the floor between us.

Not yet, young lady, I wanted to say. *What are you going to do about the small matter of falsified scientific data?* I knew my place, however, and remained silent. As I moved my feet to accommodate her briefcase, I noticed a set of gold initials in the corner—CMP—and vaguely wondered what her middle name was. I looked at the initials longer than I needed to, not clear why, but something was flitting around in my brain trying to connect itself to an important piece of a puzzle.

I almost missed Matt's next agenda item, tuning in to hear him finish a sentence.

"... and be extremely cautious, at home and at work. If you feel like you want police protection let me know."

Leder's body had been found in the foyer of his Medford home on Sunday morning while his wife was singing in the German Lutheran Church choir. As with Eric, there was no sign of struggle. Both victims had apparently welcomed their murderer.

Our general meeting seemed to be over.

"Let's take a short break, and then I'd like to talk to all of you separately. I'll take Gloria first and clear up some final details of her contract," Matt said.

You're being a little extreme, Matt, I thought, but smiled and nodded.

"It might work best if you four decide who'll be next—whoever has another appointment or whatever. It shouldn't be more than ten minutes each in any case."

"How did I do?" Matt asked when the two of us were seated back in his office.

"You sound like the former mayor of New York," I said. "But I'm sure they all think I'm off the case."

"You are off the case."

"It hasn't been twenty-four hours since I asked for another day," I said, looking at my watch. "I have until six o'clock this evening."

"Okay," he said. "We'll celebrate the official end of your contract. Let's meet at six o'clock."

I thought the little Golden Gate Bridge pin on my jacket

must be swinging from its rafters as my internal organs became unsettled. I looked at him to be sure I'd heard correctly.

"Six o'clock. Here?" I asked.

He laughed, and my bridge pin swayed in the wind.

"I don't think so," he said. "I'll pick you up and we'll find more pleasant surroundings."

As I drove home, I felt split into at least three pieces. One piece of me was thrilled at the idea of a social evening with Matt Gennaro. From another part of me, Josephine's voice warned that I might be misunderstanding his message. But the third and worst part was the frustrated voice that kept reminding me how little use I'd been to Matt's investigations.

I reviewed my meager contributions. I'd explained a little physics, which most likely had nothing to do with the murder cases. I'd caught Janice in a slipup that could easily be explained, since she may have just forgotten some September visit to the lab. I'd tracked down the Connecticut plates on the Corvette no sooner than the police had. I'd exposed poor Andrea's retrieval of her birthday present to Eric. And I'd gathered up bits of gossip that didn't amount to a nano-hill of beans.

I'd also put my money on Leder as the murderer, and he turned up a second victim.

To further indulge my feelings of incompetence, I reflected on the trouble I'd been to Matt. Because of my foolishness I'd prompted a late-night search of my apartment, including worry on his mind and dust on his jacket. Even my break-in seemed my fault. If I'd set the alarm before going out for the evening, the burglar wouldn't have gotten so far, and Matt wouldn't have been summoned to a second round of overtime.

I checked the clock on my dashboard—11:00 A.M. I still had seven hours to crack the case, and then turn myself into a gorgeous creature worthy of a night out.

All morning I had the feeling that I was very close to deciphering the meaning of the characters I'd been living with, even taking them to the bathtub with me. Something about the initials on Connie's briefcase, three characters in a row.

I thought about my options for lunch. I still had a few Girl Scout cookies in the freezer, plus garlic bread from Mangia's and one more chocolate from the box Peter had brought. I decided to make a stop for real food, including something to offer my six-o'clock guest.

I arrived home with two large sacks—fruit, cereal, juice, eggs, and cheeses from the supermarket in one, and breads and muffins from Luberto's in the other. I climbed up the stairs past the closed door of Rose's office and remembered that she and Frank were taking a rare day off together. I was grateful that Leder's body wouldn't be replacing Eric's in the main parlor, since he lived in Medford. As I kicked my apartment door shut behind me I wondered why I'd bought so much food. Was I planning on more company?

Rose and Elaine had left similar messages on my machine.

From Rose I heard, "Gloria, what's happening? I heard about Dr. Leder. Please take care of yourself and call me when you get back from the police station."

Elaine, who must have called right after the morning news in California, sounded equally concerned about me, and I tried not to take either message seriously. *After all,* I thought with a smile, *I'm going to be under police protection all evening.*

I was anxious to tell both women about what might be called my date with Matt, but decided I'd wait until I had something more definite to report. I still hadn't put Josephine's voice to rest—maybe Matt did just want to celebrate the end of my contract. Period. In the end I had to be satisfied with leaving messages on both Rose's and Elaine's machines, telling them I was fine.

I carried a plate of cheddar cheese, grapes, and apple slices to my computer table and hit the top right key to boot up my drive. As usual, the last thing I'd worked on came to life on my screen, my notes and transparencies on how lasers work.

On one of the transparencies I'd drawn two circles, one to

represent the area illuminated by a regular flashlight, and the other a beam from a laser. The flashlight's area was a much larger circle, with light spread out evenly across a wide diameter. The laser's circle of light was tiny and intense. I marked the radius of each circle, r_F for the flashlight and r_L, for the laser, and wrote the formula for calculating the areas, πr^2.

The transparency was finished except for adding π, the Greek letter pi, which represents the ratio of the circumference of a circle to its diameter, and I decided to take a minute to complete the file. To add the letter in its Greek form to my document I had to use a special menu item called keycaps. I selected keycaps, typed a regular p from the keyboard, and looked up at the screen to see that I'd produced a π on the screen.

It worked as I'd expected. But I got much more than my π. I got the last piece of the puzzle that I needed.

It finally dawned on me that if Eric had been typing Greek letters or any other special mathematical notation with his keyboard, he'd have had his keycaps selector on. So when he typed in letters to tell us who his murderer was, they appeared as keycap symbols, not the standard English alphabet. The characters could be the keycaps version of the murderer's name or initials. I realized that was why the letters on Connie's briefcase had been nagging me all day. Somewhere in the back of my brain, I'd already had the idea that Δμ∫ might be someone's initials.

I sat up in my chair, hardly able to contain my excitement. I had to work backward to unscramble the code. I kept my keycap selector on and began hitting the keyboard, watching the screen to see which symbol came up.

I started in the middle row of letters, the usual base position for touch typing. I typed ;+lkj and saw the symbol Δ when I hit the letter J. I continued typing, moving to the bottom row of the keyboard, until I saw a μ. It came on the screen when I hit the letter M. An integral sign ∫ showed up when I hit B. Δμ∫ was J. M. B. in keycap language.

Janice Bensen? I searched through my notes, nearly tearing the pages in my haste, to see if I had any record of Janice's middle name or maiden name. None. I checked the Revere phone book and found only Bensen, Paul K., who I knew was Eric's father, and Bensen, E. and J., no middle initials.

I mentally ran through my options and came up with calling Matt or Janice directly. I wasn't anxious to call either one—Matt because he might think I was faking an opportunity to speak to him and Janice because she might be a double murderer. If Leder had also figured out the code, Janice might have killed him, too. I stopped short at "If Janice knows I know . . ."

I punched in Matt's number, choosing a known non-killer over a possible murderer, and got his voice mail. Not wanting to disturb him by paging him at lunchtime, I left a message.

"This is Gloria Lamerino at one o'clock on Monday. I have a clue I think you should hear about. It might be important. Please call when you have a chance."

As soon as I put down the phone, I had what seemed like a good idea at the time. I'd call Janice and pretend to need her full name for my final report.

Another answering machine. Another message.

"This is Gloria Lamerino at a little after one on Monday. I'm writing up my final report for Sgt. Gennaro and I need to know your full name, maiden name, and place of birth. Call me when you have a chance. Thanks."

I was proud of myself for throwing in the red herring of place of birth.

Since my business was at a standstill until I heard from either Matt or Janice, I tried Rose again and reached her.

"Another murder," she said. "Gloria, I'm worried about you."

She didn't say that I could be next but I knew she was thinking it. To put her mind at ease, I told her how I'd worked out what I thought was the meaning of the characters in the printout.

"So you're sure Janice Bensen is the murderer?"

"Yes, fairly sure."

"Did you call Matt? You shouldn't be alone, especially now that you know."

"I left a message for him. Everything's going to work out fine."

Rose wasn't as relieved as I thought she should be, so I left out the part about my message to Janice, a move I was having second thoughts about myself.

"Do you want me and Frank to come by?"

"No. In fact, I have plans for the evening, with Matt," I said, figuring that was the one thing that would distract her from worrying about me.

Although Rose usually has a keen sense of justice, I knew she saw the end of the murder investigation as the beginning of my social life, and I capitalized on that to take her mind off my physical well-being. I told her how Matt suggested meeting that evening, and before I could emphasize the part about celebrating the end of my contract, Rose went into high gear.

"Yes," she shrieked into the phone. "What are you going to wear?"

"Any suggestions?"

"White Shoulders."

"A white jacket?"

"It's a perfume, Gloria, haven't you even seen ads?"

"They don't advertise in *Scientific American*," I said. "What else should I wear?"

"Nothing," she said, and we both laughed.

"I have to pick up a new candelabra near my house," Rose said. "I'll grab my White Shoulders and bring it up to you by five-thirty."

Hearing the excitement in her voice increased my own, and I went to my closet to choose my outfit. I wished I knew exactly what pleasant surroundings Matt had in mind. A walk on the beach with sensible shoes? A dark formal restaurant with shiny black sandals? A stroll through Boston Common with casual loafers? I couldn't picture Matt arriving in black wing tips, so I went for my gray suede T-straps with crepe soles. Working upwards from my shoes, I pulled out my gray-and-blue broadcloth paisley pants, which looked a lot like the runner in my entryway. I shook out the matching tunic top and hung the suit on the door.

With more than three hours before my perfume was due, I spent most of it on cleaning chores—washing my dishes, vacuuming, and changing the sheets on my bed. At four-thirty, I put on a CD of Gregorian chant and sat in my rocker, dressed for the evening except for my shoes. Between the relaxing music and the relief of having at last done something useful to Matt's investigation, I fell asleep.

I woke up, not knowing how long I'd been out, when I heard a shuffling sound outside my door. *Rose and her perfume,* I thought, *a little early.* As I stood up to go to the door, it swung open, and I realized I hadn't gone back to lock it after carting in my groceries that afternoon.

Janice Bensen stood on my threshold.

"I thought I'd deliver the information in person," she said.

Chapter Twenty-three

For one desperate moment I thought Janice might have just dropped in to tell me her middle name was Theresa and her maiden name was Jones. She was wearing sweatpants and thick athletic shoes. With a dark blue gym bag slung casually over her shoulder, she looked like any suburban housewife off for an afternoon of fitness routines. But her wildly disheveled hair and glassy, staring eyes contrasted sharply with her pink teddy-bear sweatshirt and told me that Janice had committed two murders and was contemplating a third.

"Miller," she said, and I remembered a few hours too late that Eric's father had referred to Janice's father as "old man Miller."

"Janice Miller Bensen. J. M. B.," she said. "You scientists are too smart for your own good. I always told Eric that." She seemed to be biting her lower lip as she talked and I couldn't imagine how I understood her words. "You all thought I was stupid, just a secretary, lucky to be married to an important physicist, that I'd be nothing without him."

Janice was standing on my narrow runner, about a third of the way past the threshold of the one and only door to my apartment that led outside.

"No one thinks secretaries are stupid, Janice. And we all think you've done really well at your company."

Although I believed what I said about secretaries, at that moment it didn't matter. I didn't even remember what company Janice worked for. I was grasping for any words that might calm her down.

"For years all I heard was hydrogen this, hydrogen that," she said. "It was going to make us rich. It was going to get me a family. Then he thinks first he's going to be high and mighty honest and chuck everything and then he's going to walk out on me."

Words I'd learned in my negotiating seminars and communications classes ran through my head, and I actually used one of the classic phrases on the double-murderer in my living room.

"I understand how you'd be upset, Janice," I said, showing more loyalty to sensitivity training than it deserved. "Let me help you work this out."

I came to my senses, however, and let my survival instincts take over when I saw her hand reach into her duffel bag. I took a step closer to the edge of the runner, reached down and pulled as hard as I could. Luck was on my side as I caught her balanced on one foot, walking toward me. She fell backward toward my door, her head hitting the open door, the gun falling out of her hand.

I made a split-second decision not to try to get past her, out my door. Instead I ran back to my bedroom, grabbing my cordless phone on the way. As I'd guessed she was far from knocked out by her fall and I could hear her already moving in my direction. I slammed my bedroom door and locked it behind me. I knew the flimsy lock on the knob was relatively useless, but I hoped it would at least slow her down and buy me a little time. I had no idea what good time would do me, trapped in my attic, the only place left to go. I thought of my warnings to dozens of leading ladies in movie thrillers.

"Don't go up there," I'd say to the celluloid women, gritting my teeth, but they all did, from Olivia de Havilland to Julia Roberts.

On the way to the hallway I passed my exercise bicycle and wished I'd used it more often. Not only did Janice have a twenty-five-year age advantage, she was fit in a way that I never was even at her age. *Too late now,* I thought, resolving to join the senior softball league at Disalvo Park if I lived to have the chance again.

Besides age and extra pounds, the other things working against me were my wide-legged paisley pants and bare feet. I'd kicked off my shoes while I was relaxing in my rocker. The ladder to the attic was still in place from Matt's last trip up there. Ignoring creaking knees and the stiffness in my hips, I climbed up in record time, my personal best with no shoes.

When I got through the trapdoor, I tried to pull the ladder up but Janice had already broken through my bedroom door and reached the bottom rung. Her weight kept me from pulling the ladder through the opening.

I was on my knees at the edge of the trapdoor, keeping to the side, where I hoped a bullet wouldn't find me. With my left hand, which has never been very dexterous, I was pushing 911 on my phone pad, and with my right I was struggling with the top of the ladder, trying to unhook it from the grooves in the attic floor. I mentally drew the force diagram with an arrow to represent Janice's weight on the third or fourth rung and another arrow to represent the direction I was pushing. I realized I'd need two hands to unhook the ladder completely, but I didn't want to give up my phone work. Lucky for me, Janice had only one hand available also, since she wasn't about to give up her gun.

We volleyed back and forth, grunting as if on a tennis court—just as I'd get one hook off, she'd get the other on. We were both breathing heavily and making sounds that could have passed for screams, but nothing I could distinguish, even from my own mouth. I'd given up trying to talk her out of killing me. Although Janice seemed to have abandoned her speeches about how unfair Eric and his colleagues had been to her, I heard one or two phrases from her.

"It's over," she said once, and I couldn't tell if she meant my life or hers or both.

I heard a shot ring out and shrank back from the opening. On an imaginary piece of paper in my mind, I plotted the trajectory of a bullet and got no comfort from the calculation. The next one could be dead on. At the same time I was looking around for something I could use as a weapon, remembering the baseball bat and swords I'd seen a few nights before. My deep breathing brought the sharp smell of the attic to my nostrils and I wondered if I would die among musty relics of my life.

The high-stakes interaction with Janice was straining my physical limits. I'd always been able to juggle several things at once in my mind. One spring while I was doing full-time research on crystals, I also wrote a short biography of the nineteenth-century British mathematician Mary Somerville for a children's book publisher, devised and tested a program of science experiments for first-grade teachers, and taught Italian conversation at a community adult school.

When it came to physical maneuvers, however, I couldn't successfully stir soup with one hand and hold a book with the other. I knew because the one time I'd tried it, I'd burned a large pot of lentil soup and dropped my math book, ruining several pages.

After what seemed like hours, I heard an operator's voice in my ear. I focused on my mouth and said every syllable of "Galigani's Mortuary attic" as clearly and loudly as I could. I tossed the phone to the side and grabbed the object nearest to my knees—a rubber sword. Great, I thought, feeling like a cartoon character. It was all I had nearby, however, and I slammed it down on Janice's fingers, still conscious of staying out of gunshot range. She grabbed the prop from me easily and threw it down to the hallway floor. Another gunshot frightened me into moving back from the edge, but I knew that if I left my post and let Janice's head and arm reach the opening, she'd have a straight shot at me.

The trapdoor was hinged to the floor on one side, and with the luxury of two hands free I managed to close it over Janice's hands and hold it down. The door was made of a thin plywood, however, and she pushed it up easily, but dropped her gun in the process. I heard it clank to the floor and knew I had a few seconds' grace.

I thought of all the practice I'd had with last-minute deadlines and tried to come up with a plan. I knew I didn't have the strength to keep the door down with my hands and I wasn't about to risk sitting on it and taking a bullet in my seat. I stayed at the edge, sweeping my eyes across the attic for something heavy enough to keep the trapdoor closed.

A shaft of light from the tiny attic window bounced off the edge of something shiny less than a foot away and caught my attention for an instant. My box cutter. I paused for what must have been less time than hydrogen was a metal in Eric's target chamber. I picked up the knife and removed the safety shield.

Janice was back near the top of the ladder, presumably with her gun. I twisted the knife in my hand, feeling the ribbed handle and the short blade. I swallowed hard at what I might have to do to save my life. I wished I knew more about guns, like how many bullets Janice's model held or whether guns would work after an eight-foot drop to a hardwood floor. I thought of tricking her into firing wildly, using up the bullets that were left, but I didn't have a clue how to do that.

I'd never before deliberately hurt a person physically. I was willing to risk a lot rather than use my box cutter on anything but sealing tape, but my brain was succumbing to my will to live. I took a deep breath and blocked out the knowledge that the person below me was another human being.

I came down as hard as I could with my knife, catching Janice's hands and arms. I closed my eyes and struck again and again, aware that I was meeting flesh every time. Janice screamed and so did I, but I didn't stop until I heard her fall. It was at the same time that I heard the police sirens.

Without the benefit of an anatomy class, I'd managed to slash Janice's wrists and arms and the side of her neck, enough for her to lose her balance on the ladder.

The bloody image that met my eyes when I looked down at her was more than I could bear. I fell back on the attic floor and leaned against the wall, fast becoming the most popular resting place in my apartment. Below me I heard a cacophony of sounds I'd heard only on television or in movies—police walkie-talkies, loud static, and hurried phrases about stretchers and IVs.

Blue, white, and red lights from the emergency vehicles in Galigani's driveway flashed across the dark attic, creating a patriotic image strangely like the summer's fireworks display. I stared down at my body and saw that my own hands and arms were bloody. I became aware of a sharp pain in my left shoulder and realized that one of Janice's bullets had hit me.

Before I even heard their voices, I felt the presence of Rose, Matt, and a paramedic near me in the attic. I was shivering and babbling, asking if Janice was alive or dead, not sure which answer I wanted to hear.

"She's going to be fine," Rose said, putting a blanket around me. "And so are you. He says the bullet isn't even in you."

Rose's voice had the soothing sound of a mother comforting a child who's just fallen from a swing. And whoever the "he" was that she referred to—Matt or the paramedic or God—I felt a wave of relief and a surge of confidence that I was still alive.

Rose was sitting behind me, trying to enfold my wide body within her narrow frame. Matt was in front of me, holding my cold, clammy fingers between his own warm hands. The paramedic had torn away the sleeve of my tunic top, strapped something to my arm, and dabbed a foul-smelling chemical in the vicinity of my shoulder.

"We have some surface wounds," he said in a soothing bedside voice. "Try to relax. That's it. Just one more spot."

Apparently, in my debut as an action figure I'd also slashed my own arm a few inches above my elbow.

A feeling of safety came over me as I focused on the arms of my friend around my waist, a friend who'd come to spray me with perfume. I saw the face of Matt in front of me, tender and caring, and felt the skillful hands of the paramedic at my side.

I heard the bells from St. Anthony's Church. *The Angelus,* I thought. *Six o'clock.*

"I made my deadline," I said, and listened with gratitude to the laughter of my attic guests.

Chapter Twenty-four

Matt and I sat in the Galigani living room three weeks after Janice's arraignment. Rose and Frank had invited us to dinner to sample one of Frank's specialties, pasta primavera.

Matt had been called out on another murder case just before he picked me up, but he refused to divulge a word about it. I didn't pursue the topic, hoping he would reward me by telling me more about the final resolution of the Bensen and Leder cases.

I knew that Janice had signed a confession in the hospital. I understood her frustration with Eric, even if I didn't accept her murderous resolution. After sticking with him through the long graduate school ordeal, Janice was about to be served divorce papers and for all she knew, watch Eric hook up with another woman. She knew enough about the dilemma he faced regarding the falsified data to try to make it look as though a colleague killed him.

Although Matt tried to avoid it, we'd pressured him into tying up the loose ends of the case for us.

''Janice owned two guns,'' Matt said. ''One had been her father's when he was alive, and wasn't reregistered to her. Her own licensed gun, which she'd never used, was a perfect cover.''

''Why did she kill Dr. Leder?'' Rose asked.

''He'd figured out the significance of the last three characters just as Gloria did. Janice said she'd seen Eric hit the keys in his last moment alive, but she figured that even if he wrote her name in plain English she'd taken care of it by deleting what was on the screen. Janice's plan might have worked if Gloria hadn't suggested retrieving that file.''

I covered my embarrassment by faking a slight bow from the waist as I sat in one of Rose's antique chairs, opposite Matt.

''I'm sure Leder was anxious to clear his team of suspicion of murder at least,'' I said. ''He probably confronted her without thinking of anything but salvaging what he could of their reputations.''

''And he lost,'' Frank said, shaking his head and wiping his hands on his apron.

I smelled the wonderful combination of broccoli, asparagus, green peppers, zucchini, and mushrooms and knew we were about to be called to a feast. On the sideboard I saw a white Luberto's box and guessed that was Rose's part of the meal. Matt had brought wine and sparkling cider. And, difficult as it was, I obeyed my friends' orders to bring nothing, allowing myself to be pampered while my arm was in a sling.

I felt completely relaxed, partly because I was surrounded by my friends in an elegant setting, and partly from the pain medicine I still had to take for my wounded arm and shoulder. For precaution, I'd been advised not to drive and to keep my left arm in a soft fabric holster for a few weeks.

I'd learned a few things about Matt in the time after my contract ended. He had a quick wit and a wonderful sense of humor, a degree in criminology from Boston College, and a sister with a house on the Cape. He never used after-shave and his personal car was a steel-blue Toyota Camry with a tidy interior. Although I hadn't converted him to classical music, he'd agreed to go to the Messiah concerts with me and Rose and Frank. For my part, I was letting him teach me about jazz. He loved improvisational music and knew a dozen little places in Boston and Cambridge to listen to it.

I also learned a few things about myself in the meantime, and even made a couple of real decisions, like staying in Revere, but moving to a house of my own by the spring. I started to put Josephine's negative voice respectfully to rest and thank her for her intelligence and generosity. And at some moment when he was most vulnerable to my requests and least expecting it, I planned to give Matt the little black book with Al's handwriting so we could work on it together.

Matt took my good arm, walked to the table with me, and held out a chair for me to sit on. I looked at him sideways and raised my eyebrows.

"Just until your arm heals," he said.

"Thank you," I said, and sat down next to him.

After dinner, Matt and I moved into the living room while Rose and Frank prepared cappuccinos from their shiny black espresso-maker. I walked over to the window and looked out on Adams Street, where a soft rain was falling on the immaculately groomed Galigani lawn and gardens. Mums in orange and yellow, and boxes of bright pink impatiens lined the area around their large white clapboard house. Across the street, the sight of a swing set in a neighbor's front yard and an old couple sitting on a covered porch two houses down reminded me of a Hallmark card, the family life I never had, but hoped was possible, even at my age. Not the swing set, of course, but the shared peace and contentment of people who love each other.

I turned back to the room and my eyes fell on a newspaper resting on a beautiful mahogany end table next to the couch. I saw a caption that intrigued me and picked up the paper.

Helium Reserves Sold to Hi-Tech Company, I read.

I walked toward the center of the room, paraphrasing the article as I crossed the carpet to where Matt was sitting.

"Helium is necessary for hundreds of cutting-edge products, like MRI imaging machines in hospitals and switching devices for the next generation of computers. And according to this, it looks like Dave Johnson beat out Tom Bradley in the race to get the government's supply of helium."

I continued reading until I realized that my friends weren't paying attention to me. I folded the paper and made one final comment.

''I'll bet Bradley is ready to kill him,'' I said.

''Oh, no,'' Rose said.

Matt was on his feet in a flash. He whipped the paper out of my hands and passed it to Rose, who passed it to Frank. Frank took the paper, stepped on the lever at the bottom of the plastic trash container in the kitchen, and tossed it in.

''Dessert's ready,'' he said.

''It's just an expression,'' I said, leaning over to fix the collar of Matt's shirt. ''I'm not looking for a helium murder.''